CONJURING

QUANTICO

FROM THE FEDERAL WITCH SERIES

BY

T.S. PAUL

PUBLISHED BY

ALL CHAOS PRESS

LEGAL STUFF

Read and Eat Cookbooks

Badger Hole Bar Food Cookbook

Athena Lee Chronicles

The Forgotten Engineer

Engineering Murder

Ghost ships of Terra

Revolutionary

Insurrection

Imperial Subversion

The Martian Inheritance - Audio Now Available

Infiltration

Prelude to War

War to the Knife

Ghosts of Noodlemass Past

Athena Lee Universe

Shades of Learning

Space Cadets

Short Story Collections

Wilson's War

A Colony of CATTs

Box Sets

The Federal Witch: The Collected Works, Book 1

Chronicles of Athena Lee Book 1-3

Chronicles of Athena Lee Book 4-6

Chronicles of Athena Lee Book 7-9 plus book 0

Athena Lee Chronicles (10 Book Series)

Standalone or Tie-ins

The Tide: The Multiverse Wave

The Lost Pilot

Uncommon Life

Get that Sh@t off your Cover!:
The so-called Miracle Man speaks out

Kutherian Gambit

Alpha Class. The Etheric Academy book 1

Alpha Class - Engineering. The Etheric Academy Book 2

The Etheric Academy (2 Book Series)

Alpha Class The Etheric Academy Book 3 - Coming soon

Anthologies

Phoenix Galactic

The Expanding Universe Book 2

Non-Fiction

Get that Sh@t off your Cover!

Don't forget to check the Blog every week for a New Wilson or Fergus story.

(https://tspaul.blogspot.com)

Dedications

Special thanks to my wife Heather who keeps me grounded and to Merlin the Cat, we are his minions.

CHAPTER 1

Ever had one of those days where nothing seems to go right? That's been my whole life.

My name is Agatha Blackmore and I am a witch. That is witch with a W, not a B, although I can be that, too. In the paranormal world I am what could be considered a prodigy. I cast my first spell at four, did my first transmutation at seven, and was forced to join the FBI at seventeen. My own family is terrified of me. My aunt Camilla is afraid I will turn her into a pink chicken. Again. One of these days I just might. It's her fault that I had nowhere to go and no one to train me. She called all the witch schools and told them of my little problem. The Witch Council had to step in and make me an offer I couldn't refuse. They would teach me if I joined the FBI and went to the Academy. My grandmother agreed with their plan and here I am. Fortunately for the FBI, they have really good insurance.

This is my second term with the FBI at the Academy. If they didn't need me so badly, they would have kicked me out by now. My first term was easy compared to this one. In addition to the culture shock of having actual classmates, I had to deal with other paranormal races. I'm not a racist or a classist like many witches can be. I was raised by my grandmother after my mother was hospitalized. Contrary to the belief of many in my hometown, it was not because I put her there. Daddy was killed by a drunk driver when I was six. Mom just wasn't the same after that. I accidentally created an incident at my seventh birthday party that polarized the town against me. If only my uncle had not tried to give me a unicorn. Like many young girls my age I wanted a pony. I tried to fix it. Power meet crazy. That is how I ended up with Fergus.

"Agatha snap the hell out of it! It's not your fault this time. How were you to know they were behind you?"

"Fergus, I should have checked. Magnus always said to cast a reveal spell before attempting any diagnostic of any kind. I didn't do one first!"

"Magnus? Which one was he?"

"He was the first trainer, remember, the one with the funny white hair?"

"Are you sure he wasn't the one with the hooked nose?"

"No, that was Erik. He was the German one. Magnus was the guy with the funny accent who always called me Missy."

"I think you're wrong. The Missy guy was the Texan. Mannerly or something like that. He didn't stay very long."

That is the problem right there. The FBI only had mercenaries on staff. The Witch Council had promised the FBI that they would send trainers to fix my magical problem as part of the deal that allowed me to join.

I kept breaking them.

They gave me conflicting instructions or approached my problem the wrong way. None of them were actually injured; well, except that one guy. Brady something. How was I to know the bridge by the highway had an actual troll living under it? I have to agree with Fergus though.

He did look pretty funny being chased across the front lawn by a large hairy beast.

My magic is broken. I can do little stuff, but anytime I try a large spell or something off-the-cuff, there is a fifty-fifty chance of something unusual happening. That is what happened today.

"Agatha, cast the spell exactly as I have written."

"But, Sir. Shouldn't I cast a reveal spell first? I really should check first."

"Young lady! You will do as I have asked or I will tell the Witch Council you are refusing to cooperate. Now do as I say! Cast the spell."

The instructor's name was Montgomery. Not Monte and definitely not Gomer. He resembled that old guy from the first Dinosaur movie. The one about the theme park.

"OK, Montgomery. Here goes." I cast my first diagnostic spell. It was supposed to examine the crime scene and identify any magical traces. The effect was that each foreign trace would light up and glow. It was pretty cool when he did it. I glanced at my cheat sheet and began the spell. It must have been either my pronunciation or a hand motion but something was wrong.

"Stop! Stop! You must stop! Stupid girl!" Stupid him. I was committed and had to finish the spell, even he knew that.

As I said the last word, a bright flash of light lit the field up and I heard a sound behind me that was a cross between a grunt and a screech. "Uh, oh."

I spun around just in time to see what looked like a large rabbit hop by. The animal was twice the size of a normal rabbit but now had antlers.

"What did you do? That is not the spell I gave you!" The new Council teacher was beyond mad. His face was inflamed and fire was spitting from his eyes.

"Sir, it is. See!" I held out the spell to him. He grabbed it from my hands and began checking it line by line.

"What is this notation right here?"

I peered at the line halfway through. "It looks like the word verða."

"It's not. It's the wrong tense. It needs to be umskipti. I didn't write it that way. Why is it on here?" He thrust the paperwork back at me.

"Sir, I copied it exactly from your notes."

"I do not make mistakes! You are trying to blame this disaster on me and I won't have it!" He stormed away, ranting to the heavens. I stared at the paper in my hands. We used old Norse as a modern magical language for all our spells. The word 'change' actually has five different spellings in old Norse. I guess now I know what happens when I use the wrong one.

"You just broke another one, Agatha!"

"How? I don't see what it is I did wrong! He just walked off."

"Uh, did you see the creature a minute ago?"

"Yeah it looked like a rabbit or something."

"You made another one, Agatha. That used to be a rabbit and a deer."

That horrified me. Those poor creatures. Somehow my use of the wrong word for 'change' made my magic modify those beautiful creatures. "I guess he is going to report me..."

"It's not your fault, Agatha."

I patted my shirt pocket and told Fergus thanks. I walked back to my dorm. I really needed to go to my lab and check on the experiments I have running, but it can wait a few hours. All of my magic classes were conducted on the old football field. There was very little in the way of risks of collateral damage to be had there. The school had posted signs that told of danger and death for the unwary. And those signs were taken very, very seriously. But animals generally can't read.

The Academy was set up like any military school would be. The only difference is we were in training to be law enforcement. After the Demon wars in the 1940's the FBI made accommodations for any Paranormals that wished to join. We were citizens just like other Americans. More dormitories were constructed, and the curriculum was adjusted to have subjects similar to those found at any local college. My first term was like that. Basic math, English, science, and history. Like many Paranormals I was home-schooled by my grandmother. I am not dumb. Not at all. But I didn't have a diploma or even a GED to show for my studies. The FBI is picky about that. My witch training didn't come into play until the end of the first term. The Witch Council deemed it necessary that I stay during winter break and learn to do Magic. So for the past three months it has been a never ending carousel of teachers and instructors who all tell me different things.

Classes were due to start back up in a day, so many of my friends were coming back today. I could see cars and trucks in the parking lot as I walked across the field to the dorm.

"Hey Agatha!" I waved at the trio of girls in the bright red convertible. They were sirens and triplets to boot. They were here to train to become Sea scouts. An underwater version of the FBI that only a few races could participate in. I knew of a spell or two that worked underwater. Maybe this year I could see if they would let me use them?

I heard a yell then a scream as a very large box began sliding out of a truck heading for the ground. I made a quick hand motion and hoped for the best. Off-the-cuff magic was always a bad idea, but I was learning. It was as if time stopped around the truck. Everyone was frozen including the box and those unloading the truck.

"Nice one, Aggy!"

I glanced over my shoulder at a very large man with a hairy chest and arms. He stepped up to the box and lifted it easily off the truck and set it on the ground. I just rolled my eyes. Werewolves. Always have to show off. He looked back at me and smiled. "You going to let them go now?"

"Of course. Thanks Chuck." He frowned at me. Chuck's real name was Charles Winthrop Jr. and he didn't let anyone forget it. I took Lucy's advice and called him Chuck. His parents might be scary but my grandmother was worse.

I made a dispel motion with my hand and muttered 'bak.' The people unfroze mid scream. Glancing around them they noticed the box on the ground a few feet away and us watching them. "Are you guys OK?"

Checking themselves they just stared at the box. "Chuck over there set it down for you. Are you OK?"

"We're fine... Thank you. Uh, how?"

I smiled. "Sorry, I should have said so in the beginning. My name is Agatha Blackmore." I held out my hand to the couple. Who visibly flinched and withdrew in horror. "Is something wrong?"

"Evil! Get from me, Satan!" The man made the sign of the cross and climbed into the truck. The young woman stood there for a moment as if making a decision. She turned without a word and climbed into the truck too. They burned rubber out of the parking lot. The trunk was left in the parking lot like a monolith.

"Good work Aggy, you scared off another one!" Chuck patted me on the back as he walked back to his car.

"We didn't need her kind here, anyway. Forget about it, Agatha."

All I could do was shake my head in disgust. Paranormals were revealed to the world in the early twentieth century during World War One. Since then we have been accepted by most of the mundane world: except for a few deeply religious sects, and most of the southern United States. It didn't help that on my first day of school I almost destroyed it. It was just a small misunderstanding, but it got my name in the paper in a negative way. I'm still paying for that one because it was one more reason for my family to insist I stay far away from them. Things may have ended far differently had grandmother not supplied me with her protection spells. I personally do not know how to make bullets bounce off me. Not yet. That is one of my goals this year. Provided I can keep a tutor for more than an hour or two.

The lobby of my dorm was full of returning and new students. I pushed my way through them carefully. Trying to squeeze past a couple of large beefy men I bumped one rather hard. "Sorry."

"Hey, what the hell! Bitch! Why did you just push me?"

"I bumped you. I apologized, don't go there."

The large man ignored what I said and began to turn belligerent. "I was talking to you!"

I Ignored him and continued to walk. He was about to step after me when his friends stopped him. "Idiot! Don't you know who that is?"

"She's going to be in a world of hurt when I'm finished!"

"No, you idiot! That is the school Witch! She could turn you into something."

"I already turn into a wolf! Who cares?"

"She could make you a pink wolf or turn you into a squirrel! Leave her be."

I paused at the stairwell and let the fireball in my hand fade. One thing I did have control over are offensive spells. No one touches the Witch. Not ever.

I began to climb the stairs. There were elevators, but I needed the exercise and it allowed me time to think. I lived on the second floor down at the end. As I stepped out of the stairwell, I could hear music and see my door was open.

"It smells like Cat in here. Is she back?! You said she was gone!"

"Fergus, I said she was gone for the winter. School's back now. Of course Cat is here." Catherine Moore, or Cat, is my roommate. She is a werecat and Fergus is constantly trying to get rid of her. I stepped into the room through the open door and found Cat spinning about the room singing and dancing to Lady Baba. She was dancing the 'chicken dance' as she put her clothes away. Cat was a small woman with a dancer's body. She, unlike me, was very thin and muscular. I began laughing as she stomped the beats with her feet. I knew next to nothing about modern music until last year. Cat gave me a crash course. Both mundanes and Para's had our own groups, but they crossed back and forth all the time. Lady Baba was a Russian magical group, and they wore chicken feet when they did the Yaga dance.

"Agatha! Great to see you! How was magical training?"

I reached into my pocket and removed Fergus. He stepped off my hand and onto the surface of the desk. He shook himself to get the pocket lint off his coat before commenting drolly. "She broke another one a few minutes ago!"

"Hello to you too, Fergus. How about we play a game of cat and unicorn later?"

Fergus was my familiar. Most witches didn't need the magical boost a familiar can supply. They were very rare in the modern world. Fergus has been with me since my ill-fated seventh birthday party. He used to be full sized and of the non-talking variety. For all that he was indestructible and mostly immune to magic, he was

9

deathly afraid of cats. Grandmother has a very large Savannah Cat named Zeus that thinks he is a toy.

Fergus shivered and trotted over to my coffee cup and hid behind it.

"Cat, don't tease him. You know he gets freaked out easily." She laughed at that as she gave me a big hug.

"He's in the wrong business then. So what did he mean you broke another one?" She plopped down on her bed and pulled me down with her. "Spill it Witch girl!"

I sighed and explained the whole story about the dozen or so trainers and all the problems I had had with them. Ending with the creature I made today.

"Interesting. Was it just one or did you make a bunch like those squirrels you told me about?"

"I don't know. Hopefully it was just the one. I'm sure I will be visited by the FBI administrator again."

"Ouch. He hates you! Ever since you left him hanging upside down up in the air last year."

"Yeah, I know. But no, he retired or transferred. Something. We have a new one. A woman this time: SAC Mills. The other agents say she is hell-on-wheels, but I have yet to meet her. I'm pretty sure she will make her presence known before too long."

Cat shook her head. "This year will be nothing like last year. We have weapons training, physical fitness training, and law enforcement classes. Fun!"

"You just want to get all sweaty with the coaches and the other Weres. I know how you operate, Cat. How was your winter?"

"It was great. There was a pack gathering in the Black Hills. The Native tribes allowed us to use their territory for a mass hunt and cookout. Over twenty packs participated. It was so awesome!"

"That sounds like fun. How did your pack get permission to use the land? They don't let just anyone do that." We had learned all about the tribal system and how reservation law worked in our history classes last term. Cat's pack was one of the oldest in the country. It didn't surprise me she used information she learned here.

She smiled at me. "We made a deal. Father worked it out with them but they seemed happy afterward."

Her father was the Beta in the pack. She got much of her business sense and attention to detail from him. "Did you take any pictures?"

"Of course! How could I not? I know how much you like new places." She reached into her ever present backpack and pulled out a large fat envelope. We sat and giggled like little girls for over an hour as she related her stories about the trip. The pictures were awesome.

"Cat, do you have a car this year? I ask because I need to check my lab then get some food. The cafeteria is closed today."

She made a face. "I forgot to get snacks. We can borrow Chuck's car. Dad said I didn't need it this year, too many opportunities for trouble." She put the pictures away and picked up her backpack. I stood up and walked over to my desk.

"Fergus? You coming?" I peered down into his toy barn and stall. I opened the small red door and a sound maker made a mooing noise.

"Hey! Naked Unicorn here! Can't a man have a moment's peace?"

"Fergus you're always naked. Are you coming with us or not?"

"Not; my shows on and I'm going to watch it in peace." I had to laugh. We saw the toy barn at a store that Cat took us to. I had never been inside a department store before. Fergus saw it and thought it was perfect for him to live in. When it came time to get a phone, he got one too. He used his as a television in what he called his crib. Already he was watching too much TV. The show he most liked was a cartoon about ponies.

"Hey, Chuck says get your stuff and he'll drive us over to your lab." Cat was standing in the doorway tapping her wrist.

"See you later, Fergus. I guess I won't bring you back some of that hybrid hay you like so much." I smiled; that would get him.

"Hay? I can watch the girls anytime. Wait for me!" The pocket sized Unicorn opened his barn door to the sound of Mooo! He trotted across the desk and into my hand. I placed him in my shirt pocket. I have the pockets lined with Kevlar to prevent him from filling me with holes. That horn of his is sharp.

It was the evening before the first day of classes so everyone was out blowing off a little pre-school jitters. Or as much as you can do on a Military base that wasn't exactly open to FBI students... We could hit the commissary and the PX but that was about it. If you obtained a pass, you could use the small beach facilities, but most of the coastline was for Marine corps training and exercises. Volley ball and frisbee golf seemed to be the games of the evening. Chuck was standing next to his car waiting for us.

"Hello, again Chuck! Thanks for doing this."

"You're welcome Agatha, but you know how it is. When your boss asks you to do something, you sort of have to do it."

That's true. Cat might be a tiny slip of a girl but her were-form was awesome. She was Alpha material and most of the Weres on campus knew it. Chuck made the mistake of challenging her last term and now he's her bitch! I had to laugh. That fight was a real eye-opener into the world of the Weres. Many of the big strong men all cringed like little girls when she almost bit off his fun-bits.

Chuck held open the door, and I climbed into the back seat. I usually ride shotgun, but this was a matter of ranking and position. Cat took that seat. I was just about settled when Fergus started up.

"By all that is holy! It smells like a Cat-house in here! I gave up pony play for this? Ugh. The smell is in my mouth! Make it stop."

"Fergus be quiet. The car belongs to Chuck. You remember Chuck don't you?"

"Chuck... Big. Really big cat shifter? That Chuck?"

"Yes. That Chuck."

"Hehehehehe, Chuck. How do the nuts feel, buddy? Glad you still have them?" So much for Fergus's fear of Cats.

"Fergus, leave Chuck alone. I think the badminton team still needs a birdie for their next match." Cat was peeking over the front seat at us.

"Fine. Whatever. Why is my fun always the one that gets ruined?" He snuggled back into my pocket. I could still hear him bitching. I smiled at Cat and rolled my eyes. She just laughed.

Chuck got into the car and closed the door. "OK Witchy-Poo, where to?"

I just shook my head. "Take a right out of the parking lot and head toward the base entrance."

My lab was right on the edge of the military reservation - as far away as possible from any inhabited area. The base entrance was ahead of us. "Chuck take a left at the next intersection and go five miles."

We had gone about four miles when I saw flashing blue lights in the distance. Uh Oh. Cat looked back at me. "Problems?"

I took a deep breath and let it out. Not this again. I nodded. "Chuck slow down and pull up to the roadblock."

The roadblock covered both sides of the road. My lab was just ahead on the right. From what I could see they were right on top of it, again. One of the MPs stepped up to our car and made a roll down the window motion.

"This route is closed. You need to turn around and go back that way."

"Officer, my name is Agatha Blackmore. My laboratory is just behind your roadblock and to the right. Is it possible for us to go there?" I held out my ID and pass through the window.

The MP just stared at me for a moment. Then he drew his weapon and aimed it at me

Chapter 2

My first thought was Not Again! I automatically readied both a defensive and an offensive spell. It was Cat who may have saved the man's life.

"Officer! Why are you pointing a gun at my friend?" She said it at the top of her voice. It was almost a scream. Several other uniformed MPs came out around the Humvee to see what was happening.

"Jenkins! Goddammit! Put that weapon away and step away from the car!" The officer still had me locked up and was seconds from being a crispy critter. The Sergeant approached the officer and snatched the gun out of his hands. "What in the hell did you think you were doing? We don't go around shooting at people unless they start shooting at us first! Now, why did you draw your weapon?"

The now wild-eyed officer looked at me then back at his superior. He raised his hand and pointed at me. "Witch!"

Really? I bowed my head. Why does this keep happening to me? I fixed the Sergeant with a smoldering gaze. "Sergeant? My name is Agatha Blackmore and my laboratory is over there behind you. We were on our way there." I held out my documents again but didn't let the fireball die.

The sergeant took a few steps forward and peered at my badge without touching it. His eyebrows went up, and he glanced back at me. "Hmmm. So that is your lab?"

"Yes. Let me guess. Someone or a group of someones either tried to force their way in or poked where they should not have poked. Am I getting warm?" At his look I knew I was either really close or dead on the money. "Sergeant, this has happened before. Somewhere, there should be orders regarding my lab. I know they posted warning signs after the last time over six months ago."

I could see in his eyes when he came to a decision. He grabbed his radio and called it in asking about me and the orders surrounding the lab. There was a very long pause before whoever he called got back to him.

"Sir, yes. Yes. Yes, she is right here. No, Sir. It was the witch that told me to check into the orders. No, Sir. We never thought to check. Yes. Yes, I understand. Thank you, Sir."

Both Cat and I sat transfixed by the expressions traveling across the man's face as he talked to someone higher. Cat cringed a few times telling me that she could hear the other end of the conversation. Weres.

"Miss Blackmore? I apologize for Private Jenkins. He overreacted. I have been informed that you can help us with the problem we have." I had been watching Corporal Jenkins face, and he was now sweating and pale after being called a Private.

"Jenkins get that barricade moved! Let's get this car through it." They cleared the barricade and Chuck steered for the hole they created.

"Uh, why do I smell something burning?"

Oops. I looked down and my fireball was scorching the back of his seat. I reabsorbed the magic, and it went out. "Sorry Chuck, that was me. I scorched the back of your seat pretty good. Send me the bill and I'll have it fixed. OK?"

He laughed. "No way! It gives me something to tell the boys! Were you really going to throw it at him?"

I thought for a moment. "Pretty much. No one touches the Witch. Been there done that. Never again."

We passed through the parked humvees and arrived at the edge of our destination. I could see a large group of what looked like Marines stuck in various poses around the outside of the Lab. A military police unit was stuck halfway in with its officers hanging out of the doors. Several ambulances were standing by as well as a tactical unit. I tried not to laugh.

Climbing out of the car I told the Weres to stay put. Less confusion that way. As I closed the door, I could sense the sergeant I spoke to approaching. I turned just as he was about to grab my arm. Crossing my arms in front of my body I glared at him. "Now first things first. Why were those Marines trying to break into my lab?"

"Wait. What?" His head pulled back as I confronted him. I didn't have time to say more as a Marine Major confronted me backed up by his goon squad.

"Is this her? Look here, you! How dare you put spells on my men! You are under arrest! Sergeant take her into..." As soon as he said the word arrest I froze him and his goons.

"You didn't answer my question. Why were Marines poking around my Lab?"

"Because I ordered them to." I turned and looked at the older woman in a sharp business suit.

"And they chose to ignore the signs and the warning notice on the door?"

"I told them to. We have not been introduced. My name is Special Agent in Charge Madeline Mills."

"Nice to meet you Special Agent. Now, why did you tell them to attempt to break in? They could have been killed!"

She studied me for a moment. "My predecessor left me some unreadable notes concerning this place. I rescinded the orders concerning it to see what would happen."

"Are you freaking crazy?" I saw the look on her face. "Of course you are. OK. Short story. You know about how I ended up here?"

She nodded. "It's a special program to give the bureau its own Magical Agents."

"Correct. I have a few issues with my family and the Council offered this as a solution. They have teachers coming to help train me."

She nodded. OK. At least we were on the same page so far. "My grandmother sent along some witch supplies so that I would not have to rely upon the FBI for them."

"We have many resources available to us. We can get most anything that you would need." I smiled. She did know what was in there.

"So, you do know what is in my lab."

I looked past her to a trio of men in suits peering at my lab. I could feel the magic coming off them in waves. "You might want to tell your Merc's to leave my shield alone." As I watched one of them stuck his arm inside and was unable to pull it out. "Oops. Too late."

The SAC turned and made a face as she watched the three men trying to remove the man's arm. "Where did you get those three?"

"Those are some of our best contractors! They have saved many lives."

"Uh, huh. Let's see if they can get his arm out."

The three men struggled some more and finally a second man's leg became stuck too. They were starting to attract attention from the military now.

I shook my head. "That is why you need me. Those three would kill everyone here to get at what is inside that building. My grandmother sent what I would need to protect myself and perform my duties for the FBI. Before you say anything, listen. The supplies that are available commercially are shadows of themselves. The pure forms are the real deal. Look around you if you don't believe me. This has happened before. It is why they put the signs up. While I am here on the base, the traps I set are mostly non-lethal. If I leave they are not. Only I or my grandmother can release them. They are that powerful." I turned and pointed at the three Mercs. All three were now stuck.

"How did you know they tried to break in?"

I smirked. "It is the only way the trap would have triggered. Someone has to either attack the building or attempt to get inside without a key. The wards are set to allow certain people and animals into them. As I said we have had issues in the past."

"Can you release my people?"

"Of course." I muttered a phrase to myself, careful to not speak the whole thing aloud. Some secrets should remain secret. I waved my hands and made the gesture for release. The result was dramatic.

The first to drop was the three Russian mercenaries. They were followed by the MPs then the Marines close to my building. The rescue squads rushed in along with the ambulance teams to check for injuries. I only had eyes for the Mercs. The three of them made a beeline straight for my lab. This close they would be able to sense some of what was inside.

I took two steps to my left getting the SAC out of my line of fire. "Stop." I said it loud enough for them to hear. They continued to rush forward toward the prize of a lifetime. Dammit! I held out my hand, and it burst into flame. I cried out 'halda' and took a step toward them. The taller of the three heard me and froze. He noticed my right arm.

"Ms. Blackmore what is the meaning of this! I demand you stand down!"

"Sorry Special Agent, but your hired help have scented out my stuff and now that my defenses are down they are trying to take it."

She looked at the three men as they approached the building. She yelled at them. "Vernut'sya k avtomobilyam."

They looked in her direction, but ignored her. I shook my head. It was up to me. The building had a failsafe, but everything would be gone. I needed that stuff!" They won't follow your orders. My stuff will make them kings back home and they know it. Step back please."

I spoke 'halda' again and threw a fireball at them. It exploded between them and the building. The taller Russian pointed in my direction and muttered to his companions. They spoke words aloud and began tossing spells in my direction.

Idiots! I spoke 'skjald-borg' and a shield wall formed, separating us from the mundanes. It was one of the first laws. Protect the innocent. None of their spells impacted upon me. They hit my protections and bounced off. I powered up another fireball and reinforced it with a shield of electricity. I watched as it burned through their shields and electrified the taller man. He fell to the ground in convulsions. One down, two to go.

SAC Mills strained her eyes to see inside the wall that suddenly appeared between her and the Witch. She shook her head. It may have been a mistake to send in troops to break in. Her predecessor really had left garbled instructions regarding the witch student. Her bosses had left instructions too. Test the witch. Her only experience with magic had been with the Mercenaries that the FBI hired. This girl was something else.

"Happy with yourself?" The Special Agent looked behind her. A slim young looking girl stood behind her. She was pointing at the Witch. "You do realize that if you get Agatha killed before she finishes her training the Witch Council will most likely never work with the FBI again. No matter how much you beg."

Studying the girl, the Special Agent asked who she was.

"I'm Agatha's roommate. Catherine Moore - nice to meet you. So what happened to piss-boy? He retire?"

Piss boy? "Did you know the former Director?"

"Sort of. He tried to have Agatha killed on her first day at school. He claimed it was all a misunderstanding, but she had him upside-down thirty feet in the air for over an hour. Scared the piss right out of him!" Cat was peering at her roommate through the shield.

"Chuck? Go make sure those three idiots don't have an escape route." The giant man standing behind the small girl walked over to the Merc's car and casually ripped the doors and tires off it.

Madeline swallowed and looked back at Cat. "He's handy to have around."

"He is, isn't he? Get ready, Agatha has them on the run." The three men were now trying to hide behind the MPs' car and were tossing all sorts of spells at her. Agatha was still responding with fireballs. The men suddenly ducked down low as she fired one off. She quickly tossed a blue ball that froze the entire area, including the three Mercs. Suddenly the shield dropped and Agatha Blackmore stepped over to her friend.

"Hey Chuck, good work on their car!" The large man ducked his head and blushed.

"So, Special Agent Mills. Shall we continue our conversation about my lab?"

Special Agent in Charge Mills looked at the scorched earth and the frozen Mercs on the ground. She shook her head, no. "Are they dead?"

"No, they are only frozen. The Council of Witches will have a bone to pick with those three so I'm saving them for the moment. They threw the first fireball without putting up a shield. In my world that is a major no-no. Innocent people are supposed to be protected."

"Oh, OK. Uh, what about Major Smart over there?"

I looked to where she was pointing and saw the Major and his goons. "Oops. Sorry." With a wave they weren't frozen anymore.

The Major opened his eyes wide as he realized the subject of his ire was not in front of him anymore. He stared at the empty space in front of him for a moment and quickly looked around searching for me. His gaze landed on me and the others. "Sergeant, arrest that woman!" The three military goons looked confused, but turned and headed in my direction.

I sighed and turned back toward the Director. "I'm about to piss off the Marine Corp. Do you want to handle it?"

Director Mills just stared at me. I shook my head and turned to confront the three Marines. At the last minute Chuck and Cat stepped in front of me.

"Hey, what are you doing? This woman just saved your asses! Don't listen to that bozo."

The three Marines stopped and stared at the two in front of them. They started to push through when Director Mills snapped out of whatever transfixed her. "Freeze! I am FBI Academy Director Mills and these people are under my command. Tell Major Smart that he cannot arrest MY people."

The resulting argument lasted for over an hour. More Marine Brass was called in and now Director Mills was under the microscope as General Varmkorv yelled at her for breaking procedure and rescinding orders without his knowledge. The general was a large imposing man with white hair. The air around where the conference was happening practically shivered with each scathing yell. I found it quite interesting, actually. The only way that would happen naturally was if the person yelling was a paranormal of a certain persuasion. It made me wonder how a Frost Giant managed to become a Marine General.

Through it all I sat on Chuck's 1971 green Buick Riviera trying not to leave any marks on the surface. You could tell he loved that car. It was carefully polished with imported car wax every week. The unusual humped back part of the trunk was scratch free. It was a very unique looking car. Chuck claimed he saw it in an old television show and just had to have it. His father helped him search the internet and sales rags across the country to find one.

The field across from my lab usually had a top growth of clover and foot-high weeds on it. I could see none of that. What I could see were three medium-sized animals similar to rabbits eating every green leaf in sight. As they moved, I could glimpse the antlers on their heads. It made me wonder how far exactly that spell had traveled. Somehow I just knew that was going to come back and bite me in the ass.

"Watcha looking at girlfriend?" I shook my head and looked to my right. There was Cat and Chuck; she had a goofy grin on her face.

I pointed at the field. "I was looking at the..." The three animals were gone. "I was looking at the field. It looks like they cut it early this year."

"You need to get out more if cut grass make you happy. We can probably go inside soon, the general is winding down."

"Oh? How do you know that?" I glanced in the direction of the Director's car. From what I could see he was still yelling at her.

Cat tapped her ears. "The ears hear all and know all. It will be over in a minute. Bet on it."

As we watched General Varmkorv said his last few words and left Director Mills standing next to her car. His men gave orders to the last of the MPs and they all cleared the area. All that was left were the three frozen russian mercenaries, us, and Director Mills.

She looked at the three of us and shook her head. "I need to apologize to you three. I put you into needless danger. I have been informed that had I asked, the General himself would have given me the 'lowdown' on the magical situation." She looked at me. "Can you tell me what happened last time? The General wouldn't say."

I chuckled. "That may be why you were left in the dark. Your predecessor was not a fan. When he got word that I was coming to work for the FBI he initially was happy and passed the word to welcome me. It was like a game of telephone gone wrong. His assistant passed it to the next one and so on. When I arrived they tried to place me under arrest and grabbed me."

SAC Mills visibly winced. "What happened?" Her voice was noticeably lower.

"About what you would expect. I left the building, they shot at me. If Grams hadn't equipped me with protection spells, I might not have survived. They were not very happy with me. The director himself came down to get to the bottom of the destruction. In my own defense I did try to explain what had happened to me."

"What did he do?"

"It's more of what he said. He didn't recognize who I was and called me a little girl. I was already pissed off, so he found himself upside down about thirty feet in the air. His guards too."

I smiled. It had been really funny. "The agent who recruited me showed up and took care of the issue. Apologies were made and I eventually let the man down. But not before he pissed himself. He earned the nickname 'piss boy' from those of us in the Para community here on base."

"You didn't really call him that, did you?" She was cringing.

"Just a couple of times. He got his revenge though. I don't mean this mess either. He broke FBI protocol and gave several interviews in the local and national press describing how out-of-control I was and naming me to the press."

SAC Mills nodded. "That makes a certain amount of sense. I understand now why he trashed the files so much. He was on the way out and he knew it." She looked at the three mercenaries. "What did you mean when you said they broke the rules?"

I just shook my head. For a government organization they were so dumb. I was about to answer her when Cat did it for me. "There are rules. Even we know that. The FBI gets us to join and help you police other Para's but you still don't understand. The rules were set down over a century ago. Each race must follow them. For magical users they are to protect the innocent or the mundane whenever possible. That rule was in place before the Purge. Those three cast at Agatha without regard to all the soldiers and other mundanes around here. Didn't you notice that the first thing she did was cast a shield spell?"

"What will happen to them?" She looked back in their direction.

"No idea? If I didn't report them Cat or one of the other Para's could report me for not doing my own duty. It's a matter of survival. We police our own for the most part."

She looked at the three of us. "I don't understand. Why did they attack you in the first place?"

"Before I answer, why did you bring them with you?"

"They are part of my protection detail. The bureau pays them to assist with magical investigation. They swore they could break the spell."

I snorted and shook my head. "That spell is one of Gram's. The Council would have a hard time breaking it. The reason they attacked was they wanted my stuff. They could sense it. There is a reason I have a lab way out on the edge of our assigned area. Come on, I'll show you." I began walking toward the building. Reluctantly Director Mills followed me.

Up close the door to my laboratory looked like any other building in the area. It followed basic military construction from the mid-twentieth century. Blocky and boring. I inserted my key and opened the door.

"That's it? Just a simple lock?"

"Not quite. I turned off most of the security features. Greenhouse first. I need to check on the plants and pick up some hay for Fergus."

"Why do you have a greenhouse?" The director stared in shock as I opened the door to wonderland.

CHAPTER 3

I have always loved Gram's garden and had long wished for a garden of my own. Now I had it. With a little judicial use of witchcraft and herb magic I was able to transform the broken down commercial greenhouse into a tropical paradise. All I needed was a few tropical birds and someone to bring me a drink with a little umbrella. Too bad Fergus had to ruin it for me.

"Where's the hay? I don't smell hay! You said there was going to be hay!" Up until now the little terrorist had been very quiet. He knew not to distract me while I was fighting the Russians.

"Miss Blackmore, why is your pocket talking?"

I glanced to my right to see Director Mills staring at me. Her eyes were pinched together, and she was squinting at my upper body. I started laughing.

"I'm sorry Director, I guess you don't know about Fergus." I reached into my pocket and pulled out the Unicorn. The Director recoiled back from my hand.

"What? Never seen a Unicorn before? I could give you some horn, chicks dig the horn. It's my best feature!" Fergus started strutting back and forth across my open hand. Director Mills had her head cocked to one side as she stared at my familiar.

"Technically, Fergus here is my familiar. Most modern witches don't bother with them anymore. He was sort of an accident and has been with me since I was seven. Fergus stop showing off, she isn't interested in your horn."

The mini Unicorn looked up at me and stamped his hooves. "Fine. Whatever. Where's the hay?"

I stepped to my right and opened up a Plexiglas cover. Inside was a small bed of what looked like grass.

"Hay! Gimme gimme gimme! Agatha put me down! Please!" I shook my head ruefully and set Fergus down in the middle of the small field.

"Don't eat too much! You'll make yourself sick." The Unicorn was doing a strange little dance as he galloped around the field.

I turned back to my friends and the Director. "Unicorns."

All three of them were staring at me. "What? Is there a bug on me?" I started checking myself.

"Agatha, there's no bug. Me and Chuck want to know if you tell him bedtime stories too?" She laughed at me.

"I still feel a bit guilty for his size. I mean it's been almost eleven years since it happened but he could be off chasing other Unicorns. Instead he hangs out all day with me."

"What did you do?" I looked back at the Director.

"It's not in my files? I assumed you knew my story."

"Your files are incomplete; that is one of the factors that caused the mess outside. I am sorry about that, by the way. Director Offenberg either changed your records or never filed them properly."

"Offenberg! That was what his name was! I could never remember. Fergus just called him piss boy. In answer to your question, I was given Fergus as a seventh birthday present by my Aunt Camilla. Unicorns are suppose to be a status symbol for young witches. I refused the present and told them I wanted a pony instead. I zapped him myself and he gained the ability to talk. It appears that Unicorns like to cuss. They like to cuss a lot. So I tried to fix it. And then he got smaller. There is a bit more to it but that is the basics. If you want the whole sordid truth of it all contact my Grams or the Witch Council, they can tell you."

Waving off the matter, I spread my arms. "This is the greenhouse! When they gave it to me half the glass was broken and the watering systems didn't work. After I got it fixed, I started up my garden. My family coven and circle are composed of what might be called classic, or herb witches. Or at least the older members are. I was home-schooled by my grandmother. She taught me everything she knows about Earth Magic. Much of what Grams does is magic of that style. Potions and charms work very well in the right hands. Many of the ingredients needed for such concoctions are rare and costly. An Earth witch will have an extensive herb garden and many contacts to get the things that she needs. When it was agreed that I would be coming here to school she made sure I would be able to have the things I would need to do my job."

"Wait, so all of this is magical?" The Director looked around at the various plants and flowers in wonder.

"Most of it is. Even the hay greedy guts over there is in has magical properties." Fergus was sound asleep in the middle of the bed of hay snoring.

"Most modern or non-trad's buy their ingredients off the Internet. Many of the magical properties are washed out and have lost strength by the time they get them home. My garden can be very powerful in the proper hands."

"So the Russians wanted a garden?"

"Sort of. There are a few plants that are so rare that many in the community think they are mythical. They can be sensed if you know what you are looking for. I have a few other things next door too. Come on, let me show you." I waved them over to the door. A short hallway connected the greenhouse to the warehouse. My lab was on the far side.

The warehouse was more of a garage. A large reinforced steel roll-up door was at one end of the room. It was secured to the floor with chains and very large locks. Several large eye-bolts were sunk into the concrete ensuring the door did not roll up. A small pile of crates sat at one end. Long tables covered in clear plastic cases dominated the room. "This is my primary supply cabinet. Each of these boxes hold herbs and other materials that allow me to make certain spells and formula."

Cat and Chuck had been here before so to them this was old news. The Director walked up and down the aisle of tables and peered at the snap-tight boxes. "What's in here?" She reached for a box.

"Be careful with that one, Director, it is a very powerful aphrodisiac. It can bring love back into your life if prepared properly." The Director froze and then very slowly opened the box. Inside was a bag of dried leaves and flowers along with fresh flowers held in a magical stasis.

"They look like hops. So delicate. What is it?" She was gently stroking the leaves and flowers.

"Origanum dictamnus or Dittany of Crete. It only grows in a certain part of Crete up in the mountains. You have a good eye. It's in the hops family of herbs. This little beauty is traditionally a healing herb, but it makes a good present for newlyweds to spice up the wedding night. The Greeks value it as something to be used for love." I gently closed the box and smiled at the Director. "I'm going to guess that you garden a bit."

"My family are farmers and Dad plays at brewing his own beer." I nodded.

"Through there is my lab. I make potions and other things so I can practice my witchcraft." I pointed to the other door. "The FBI get me as an agent and they get my skills. But all of this is mine. I can't be effective without it. All of it is why those three attacked me. Some of this would set them up for life back home."

"You said that before, outside. What do you mean by that?"

"Let's go into the lab. I have a small kitchenette where we can sit down." I opened the door and led them into my lab. Off to the side was a small round table and four chairs. A refrigerator and microwave sat in the corner. "Chuck, there are some nuker meals in the cabinet over there if you're hungry."

The large Were strode over to the counter and grabbed a snack.

"Cat, I have soda and water in the fridge."

She opened the door and pulled out a couple of drinks. "Director?" She held up a soda.

"Diet if you have it. Thank you." Cat set a bottle of water in front of her.

"The FBI hires Merc's to take care of magical stuff for them. Do you know why?"

She stared at me with a puzzled look on her face. "What do you mean why? The Witch Council won't provide help so we have to hire from outside."

"I'm sorry, what I meant to say, was why only hire Russians?"

"That I don't know. We have a list of help that we can call on to aid in investigations. I don't understand how you could take out the three of them alone. They are some of our best hires!"

I sighed. "I had a similar conversation with Director Offenberg. He didn't believe me or at least I don't think he did. Russian magic users took a real beating in the Demon War. The Rodnover priesthood was controlled by the volkhvy. Call them priests or priestesses. It was they that paid the highest price in stopping the 'Madman of Berlin.' They burned themselves out in a magical distraction that allowed the English Witch Council to strike directly and bypass the Demon Prince's protections. Their loss spelled an end to the theocratic rule in their country. Stalin took over and we now have what the country became. The magic users lost their teachers and their leaders all in one fell swoop. They have no Council to stop them from whoring themselves out to the highest bidder. They are diminished but refuse to believe it. I told your predecessor that hiring them was a mistake. They will do as you ask of them but that is all. They really only look out for themselves unless you pay them heavily. Pure mercenaries. With them nothing is free." I paused for a moment. "I have a bit more juice than they do. But magic is magic. I have had better teachers and have access to better components." I waved at the greenhouse.

"You said training. Why is the Council sending trainers to you here?"

"Boy, he really didn't like me did he if he left all that information out of my files? To quote Fergus, my magic is lopsided. My first spell broke records. I changed a bunch of squirrels at age four. I had my accident with the Unicorn at seven and I have done a few other things. Spells such as protection or the basics I can do just fine. It is when I have to concentrate upon something or don't think things through that accidents happen. It was part of the deal in my coming here. Many in my family are afraid that I will accidentally change them. They informed the witch schools of that fact. Only the FBI would take me. But you had to agree to teach me the basics of law enforcement and allow the Council to send magic trainers. They claim they can fix me."

"How many teachers have they sent?"

I heard a smirk from the far corner of the room. Ignoring my recalcitrant roommate I continued on. "After this morning over a dozen. I keep breaking them."

"OK. That explains the overly excited elderly man I had in my office this morning. He made no sense whatsoever, but kept repeating that it was not his fault. What did you do to him?"

"I still don't think I was wrong. He was trying to train me to do a diagnostic spell that would trace magical sources. He claims I wrote the wrong word down in my book."

"Wrong word?"

"Most wizards or witches perform magic in a different language. We could do it in English but the use of the different language makes it more of a ritual than everyday practice. Generally, we use Old Norse. There are some that use Latin or Greek. I prefer the Norse. The word actually has five different spellings that mean essentially the same thing. However if used in a spell different things can happen. That was news to me, actually."

"What did you do to upset him so?"

"One of the many teachers they have sent told me to always cast a look-around spell before casting. Just to make sure that there were no bystanders or innocents that can possibly be harmed. Montgomery, the old guy, told me that spell was unnecessary and to do what he told me to do. So I did. He began yelling at me as soon as I spoke the wrong word. The diagnostic failed to happen and there was a bright flash of light. Behind us on the edge of the tree-line a rabbit and a deer had literally just stepped out as I cast. Somehow the spell fused the two creatures. We now have at least one Jackalope here on the reservation."

The director smiled and then when she realized I wasn't kidding, grimaced. "Why do you say at least one?"

"I think I sort of saw three earlier in the field across the street. The last time I did something like this was when I was four. Those squirrels are still purple. I have no idea how far that spell may have gone. I'm sure the Council will be contacting you before too long. I half expected to hear from them before I ran into your trio of Russians."

"About them. Will the Council send someone?"

"Well, I sent them the required message after I froze them. They usually respond within twenty-four hours.

Think of them as cable repairmen. The spell will hold until they show up."

Director Mills looked at me and then at Cat. "What am I to do with the three of you?"

"We would like for you to let us be students, ma'am. It's why we're here. Think of us as natural resources. We just need training to make us more useful."

"I know school hasn't started yet, but I want all of you to keep low profiles from now on. This incident is going to make waves. I will take responsibility for most of it, but there could be repercussions. Be careful. Now I need to get back to my office. My assistants must have thought the world ended or something by now."

Locking down my lab I scooped up a still unconscious Fergus and exited the building. I muttered to myself as we walked. The protections and the wards surrounding my building slowly began to reform and expose themselves. When we reached the three Russiansicles I telekinetically moved them to the other side of the road laying them in the field. "It wouldn't look good to have the whoever the Council sends get stuck in my wards..." I muttered.

As we reached her car, I triggered the last of the wards. The lab was now protected again.

"I will reissue the orders concerning this place and notify the Marines. I expect to be notified if there are any more accidents. Am I understood?" We all nodded. "Good. Enjoy your classes tomorrow; I will be watching."

Cat looked at me as Mills drove away. "Agatha, we are in big trouble."

I nodded. "Yes, yes we are. But we're tough and we can handle it."

"Or we just send Chuck in our place and let him deal with it."

I smiled at her. "Good plan. Let's do that one."

Chuck looked up at the mention of his name. "Hey now, what am I doing?!"

Chapter 4

Picking up my schedule was far easier than it had been the previous year. Gone were the guns and agents shooting at me. I found I almost felt a bit neglected! As I climbed the steps I glanced around at the brand new entranceway and reception desk. The damage hadn't been much but in the end they replaced the whole thing. It made me wonder what sort of defenses it now contained. Were they the same as the old ones? Or better...? The blonde behind the desk flinched when I gave her my name, but she didn't attack me like last time. It boggled my mind why in an age of digital communications we even used hard copy class schedules. It had to be some sort of government bureaucracy thing.

"Miss Blackmore, here is your class schedule. Director Mills left a note here for you to see her this morning. According to her calendar, she is available now. Do you have any questions about your classes?"

My head was swirling. I just saw the Director yesterday. I got my eyes to focus and looked at the paper I had clutched in my hand. Law enforcement procedures three times a week in the morning, followed by martial arts and phys-ed. Two days a week I had target shooting and basic combat. In the afternoons my schedule was marked 'special' with a symbol I was unfamiliar with. I looked up at the mousy blond and asked. "What does this mean on here? Special, with this symbol?"

"That is why the Director needs to speak to you. Shall I tell her to expect you?" I looked at her. Her fake smile really made me nervous. Well, that and the fact that her right hand stayed under her desk the entire time. What did she think I was going to do?

"Tell the Director I'm on my way." I could see her visibly relax and actually remove her right hand from whatever she had it on.

Shaking my head, I headed up to the second floor. Several agents and security guards passed me on the way, all of them clutching at their sidearms. I considered taking the stairs but got on the elevator instead. Two agents stepped on with me and ignored me. They were talking to each other but kept checking their guns the entire ride up. I got off at the second floor and so did they. The Director's office was at the end of the hallway. I could sense that everyone was watching me as I stepped up to the door and knocked.

"Come." I opened the door and stepped inside. I had to shake my head. I'd been here a half year already, and these people were all still scared of me. The secretary was a youngish man who stood with his hand on his hip as I stepped up to his desk. "My name is Agatha Blackmore. Director Mills is expecting me."

"Go right in Miss Blackmore." He took his hand off his sidearm and sat back down at his desk and went back to whatever he was working on.

I opened the door and stepped inside. The Director smiled at me and started to say something. I cut her off. "What is it with all the people in this building? Every single one of them looks at me as a threat and grabs their guns. You do realize that if a member of the Witches' Council ever visits they will take offense at that, right?"

"I'm sorry, what? What do you mean they grab their guns?"

I looked at her incredulously. "Really? Have you watched any of the building security footage?"

"I haven't. Should I?"

"Not to tell you how to do your, job but if I was my Grams, you wouldn't have a building to sit in. She would have leveled the place. They act like I'm going to attack them. That mess last year? They fired first. I didn't attack anyone until those idiots in the Humvees started shooting at me."

She just stared at me for a moment. "Hold that thought." She pressed a button. "Spence? Do we have access to building security tapes from my office?"

"Uh, no Ma'am. Those can only be accessed from the security division's office."

Looking back up at me she said. "Feel like a field trip? Come on, let's go watch a movie." She took her sidearm out of a drawer and holstered it. She grabbed what looked like a tablet and her phone.

Spencer looked up as we walked by. "Spencer, I'll be out of the office for a short while. Only send the most urgent items to me. Thanks."

She turned to me as we stepped into the hallway. "I've been trying to get out of there all morning. I asked for you today to explain your schedule to you. Besides your regular classes would you be willing to teach agents and others about witchcraft and magic? Just general information and how things work, not the practical part."

"That's a really good idea, Director. When I first got here last year, I was incredibly surprised how ignorant this agency is about the paranormal world and magic. After a hundred years you would think people here would know some stuff by now. I will need to ask permission of the Council, but I don't see why they would say no."

"Great. Turn left up here." We had been walking down the hall and up a flight of stairs as we talked. As we entered the hallway on the left, we passed a sign that said security offices.

The Director stopped at the reception desk and told them she wanted badges for two.

"Of course, Director. Who shall I put for the second one?" The security officer looked at me curiously.

"Agatha Blackmore."

The guard froze in the act of typing it in and stared at the Director. She glared at him. "Is there a problem?"

"Uh, no Ma'am. No problem. Are you sure Ma'am? She's one of those." He made a hand motion.

The Director looked at me and rolled her eyes. I stifled a giggle. "She's what, Officer? A student? A woman? Oh I get it, she's a witch. We don't discriminate around here, you know? But we do represent the government. Give me the badges, please! Now."

The security officer paled and quickly made up the badges. His hands were shaking when he handed them over to her. She handed me one and turned back to the officer. "Pick a day next week and report to human resources for race relations training. I will tell them to expect you, Officer Nixon."

I clipped the ID to my shirt and followed the Director through the security scanner. It immediately went off. She started to hand over her weapon and the guards stopped her.

"Ma'am it's not that sort of scanner. Is there any item in your possession of a magical nature?"

Once again she glanced back at me. I really couldn't help myself this time. "Told you so."

"The young lady with me is of a magical nature. Allow her to pass." She motioned for me to pass through the portal.

"Ma'am, our instructions are to not allow…" He never got to finish his statement.

"Who am I? What is my position in this agency and building?"

"You are the Director."

"Who issued those orders that you are blindly following?"

"They came from your office, Ma'am."

"They did? Interesting. When did they come from my office?"

"Last year after SHE nearly destroyed the building!"

The Director turned in my direction. "Did you really?"

"No. I sort of wanted to go to school here. They fired first, and the ricochets did a small amount of damage in here. I took it outside."

She turned back to the security officers. "As you well know, Director Offenberg was retired for cause. I will review his orders to you, but you will allow us to pass. Is that clear?"

"Yes, Ma'am. I understand."

"Excellent. Now get with Officer Nixon over there. He is going to a training session on race relations down in Human Resources. I will be notifying them of your attendance. Now get out of my way!"

She passed the portal with no problems but I set the thing off. An alarm began screaming and agents popped out of doorways with guns drawn. The Director didn't look amused. She turned back around and glared at the security officers who shut the system down and sent some sort of all-clear signal.

"I'm starting to see the problem you're having, Agatha. Come on; I have some more heads to collect." I stuck close to her as we walked the hall. This was actually sort of fun in a morbid way. It was nice to actually have someone on my side for a change around here.

There was a pair of double-doors in front of us with the words 'No Electronics Allowed' prominently displayed on the doors. A row of lockers stood next to the door. The Director took her phone and tablet and placed them inside. She also took off her watch. I followed her lead and placed my phone and tablet inside her locker. My watch was of the pocket variety and very old. It had belonged to my grandfather, and I used it in my spell work.

The room inside was similar to a casino's surveillance room. Screens were everywhere. Specialized agents sat and stared at the screens making notes or notifications. No room was sacred. I nudged the Director and pointed to a camera inside her office. Her eyes suddenly got that evil glint I had seen before. Just as she was about to yell at someone I saw another violation. Cameras in the dorm rooms! I felt a small fireball form in my hand for just a moment before canceling it. Our eyes met, and she nodded. She would fix this.

The agents in the room were completely unaware of the chaos that was about to descend upon them. The man in charge of the room was sub-Director Richard Jonson. His head was down as he studied one of the students in the dormitory. He had been watching, for security purposes of course, for the entire day, when he was yanked out of his chair. Suddenly on the floor he looked up at the angry face of his boss Director Mills.

"What is the meaning of this?" She pointed at the bank of screens covering the dorm and his own project.

"Ma'am we have to search for security threats! The previous Director..."

"Was relieved for cause! This is outrageous! Do you realize the lawsuit that could come from this? They would own this school!"

"No one can sue the Government and win. It doesn't matter."

"Did I ask for your opinion? I want it shut down! Right freaking NOW!"

"Ma'am I need authorization to shut down an ongoing investigation into..."

"Agatha can you?"

I twitched my finger and a ball of electricity hit the bank of monitors and fried every single one of them in a bright flash.

"Now. I want all tapes, all records and every piece of paper or record ready for review. Right Now!" Smoke alarms began to sound as acrid smoke started to fill the room. I reached into my pocket, threw a pinch of salt and herbs on the monitors, and muttered a few words in old Norse. The fire that was about to start stopped and the room suddenly grew very cold.

"Sorry, Ma'am. Thermodynamic reaction. It will pass in a moment."

"Agatha, step outside and bring me my phone and tablet please." I nodded and did as she asked. The leader of that band of misfits chose that moment to object and her yell could be heard through the door.

When I stepped back inside most of the monitors were now shut down and the techs suitably cowed. She took her things from me and immediately called in reinforcements. I suspected it was going to be a very long day for this corner of the building. She finally dismissed me and admonished me to remember to turn in my badge at the desk.

My passage back through security was easy as making pie. The rest of the building was still the same. I suspect that she would take care of that too. All the way back to the dorm I searched for cameras. Now that I knew what to look for I was seeing them everywhere. I could see the need in public places and high security areas. But the dorms? I would take care of some of them.

The hike across campus was pleasant even though I was searching for cameras. It was only a short few weeks past Imbolc and the Oak King still reigned supreme. I speculated to myself whether I could bring Cat and Chuck into the old religion. Ostara wasn't all that far off. I hadn't thought to invite them to my rites the previous year. Several members of the ad hoc Pack were here and called my name. I waved as I entered the main entrance to my dorm. Rooming with one of the Alphas had its advantages. There was a camera in the doorway but I left it alone. Same for those on the ground floor in the main rooms and stairwells. They needed those for security. I zapped the camera in the locker room and shower areas immediately. I had to walk the entire dorm, but I killed all the bathroom cameras. The individual rooms were another issue. Stepping outside I found the junction box where all the lines exited the building. A snap of my fingers fried the whole system. I hoped that only the security department had access to those feeds.

Cat and Chuck were arguing when I stepped into the room. I looked at my two friends. Both had cat eyes and whiskers popping out of their faces. They were both seconds from changing. "Hey! Knock it off!" I yelled at the two of them.

Focusing their attention on me prevented the change. I really didn't want to listen to Fergus bitch about two really big cats in the room. He only tolerated the two in human forms.

"What is it this time?" I asked them as I scanned the walls looking for my prize.

"She won't take the title of Alpha publicly!" Both of them were now watching me stare at the walls. Cats.

"So, you thought of goading her into changing... and then what? She would see the error of her ways as she ripped you a new one? Is that what you thought? She might bite them off this time." He made a face and crossed his legs. I shook my head and laughed at him.

I wasn't having any luck finding the camera, so I said a word of power and swirled my hands above my head. Strands of color began to form. I had what looked like a ball of colored yarn floating above me.

"Agatha, whatcha doin'?" Cat was mesmerized by the colors and the swirling motion the ball was making.

"That's a good way to catch Weres. You need to remember that one, Agatha." Fergus was standing on my desk watching,

I concentrated for a moment and visualized what I wanted to happen. The ball of 'yarn' broke into a thousand strands that flew in a dozen directions. They clumped up in three locations. The light feature at the center of the room, a spot above the door, and another above the windows. Three balls of molten fire formed in front of my eyes. With a word they homed in on the spots of color and incinerated them. Shards of the light feature sprayed in all directions. Fortunately it was plastic. "Oops."

"What the hell, Agatha?"

It took me over an hour to explain. Cat kept having me go back over information concerning the Director and the camera system.

"So where is the junction box located at?" Chuck didn't look happy at all.

"It's at the rear of the building where the cable and other electrical stuff comes in at. The one I fried on this building said 'TelcomSyS High Power - Do not touch' on it."

Chuck nodded. "I will get some of the boys to help but we need to take care of the rest of them."

"I can zap a few of the individual cameras, but do you realize how many there are? I can't get them all."

"Agatha, we can sniff out cameras now that we know what to look for. The Paras can at least be protected. We are used to this sort of crap. So much for thinking this place is any different."

"Guys, chill. Director Mills had no idea they were doing this. Her first words were to shut it down. When they wouldn't she had me zap them. I think a lot of it was the old director. You both know how much he hated Para's and me."

"She's probably going to yell at me for telling others about it though. I'll take all the blame. They really need me. I doubt they will expel me over this. What worries me is some overzealous idiot like that sub-director, Richard Jonson, doing it again while we are away."

"Wait, that was really his name? Dick Jonson is his actual name?" My Unicorn was now upside down laughing uncontrollably.

"Why is that funny?" Cat shrugged her shoulders, and we both looked at Chuck. He was smirking and soon joined Fergus in laughter. Men.

"Can you make it so cameras don't work in here?" Cat looked anxious too.

"I can try. I don't have a shield spell handy so it might be dangerous. The various Council Mages have been teaching me. Let me meditate on it for a moment."

I sat on my bed cross legged and considered the problem. I can cast temporary shield spells that block all communication or intrusion. Mine are finite though. I would need energy and strength to give it structure. For the basic framework I thought I might be able to use the internal electrical system and the wooden studs. This would be one of my first off-the-cuff spells in years. Even though I was planning what I was going to do, there was no spell to work with.

"OK, I think I have a clue here. There is no spell for this in my book so I have to wing it."

"Oh, just kill me now. Please don't make me into a squirrel!" Fergus was now moaning.

"Fergus, if you won't lend me your support, just go hide in your barn." He scuttled off to his little red house with a Mooo! preceding him as he went inside.

"As I was saying. I will cast a circle in the center of the room. If you two are in it with me, you should be safe. Or you can leave the room."

The two looked at each other. "We trust you Aggy. We will stay in here with you if that's OK?"

"I love you guys." I stepped over to my desk and grabbed a few spell components and a small goddess statue.

They each gave me a hug and sat at my feet in the center of the room. I quickly called the quarters asking the four elements for their permission and protection from harm. In my mind I visualized a circle forming around the three of us. I called upon the goddess Freya to bless and protect us in upcoming battles. In my mind I traced the structure I wanted and used the power system coupled with sunlight energy to extend the spells life. I opened my eyes and received a shock to my system.

My magic was visibly penetrating the walls and floor. I could see the formula and symbols of my magic as it swirled about changing the physical structures of the walls. I looked down at my two friends. They had very large eyes and Chuck whimpered once. They could see what I was doing!

Sensing that it was time to speak my words of power I threw up both hands and forced the magic in the room to pour into the walls.

I spoke.

"Skjald-borg!"

There was a bright flash of light that blinded all of us for a moment.

"By Jewel's pointy horn, I'm not purple!" Fergus burst out of his home and began doing some elaborate dance on my desk.

"Did it work?"

I looked down at Cat and smiled. "I don't know. It was pretty cool though. I know you could see it."

"Agatha, I knew you were powerful but wow! Father has a wizard that works for the Pack. His spells are nothing like That! He doesn't have a tenth the power that you do."

"Uh, thanks? Chuck can you check the walls? They should be able to take at least a punch: it's supposed to be like a force field."

The large Were stepped over by the door and gave the wall a sharp punch. Clang!

51

"Hey, the wall's metal now?" He checked the door; it clanged too but did open.

"Thank the Goddess!" We could have been trapped inside the room.

"I wonder where I made the mistake?" I thought about it for a moment. "At least we're safe now. If they try to install something we will know it."

We now lived in a large metal room. It really was pretty cool and my magic didn't make anyone into a pink chicken. Maybe I was finally learning. The downside to it all was I now had to tell both the Council and the Director of my oopsy.

CHAPTER 5

My morning the next day started very slowly. Every resident in the dorms found a note under their doors explaining that a clerical error had postponed classes by one day and to enjoy the day off. Cat just sat up in bed, listened to what I had to say, then passed out again. Just like a Cat. I sat on my bed and meditated on my spell work the previous evening. Breaking it down I couldn't see what I did wrong or even if it was wrong. I picked up my cell phone and gave Grams a call.

"So, what is your question child?"

"Uh, good morning Grams? How did you know it was me?" I actually pulled the phone away from my ear and stared at it.

"I was notified by the Council that they detected several magical surges near Quantico and I assumed it was you. Any pink chickens this time?"

I smiled and bowed my head. There was the grandmother I grew up with. "I only use that threat for Aunt Camilla."

"What happened, Aggy?"

For several minutes I gave her the background about the Russian mercenaries and the problems within the FBI administration building. Then I told her about the surveillance and cameras.

She blew up.

"That is outrageous! The Council needs to be informed. Child, if you wish to come home I will convince the town to let you!"

"I took care of it, Grandma. The new director is pretty nice, at least to me. She was as outraged as you are. I took care of the cameras here in the dorm and had some of the Pack take out the others. The reason I called was I had a small 'oops' when I tried to shield the room. I wanted a permanent shield that would stop most threats, but I didn't have a spell for it. I made one up and it had an unexpected effect."

"Aggy dear, you know what happens when you do off-the-cuff magic. You should have called me. We could have figured something out. What happened? Are you OK?"

"I'm fine and so are Cat and Chuck. They were in here with me. Did you know that Weres can actually see magic?"

"Yes, I did. Only the really strongest can see the actual working. The rest just see color changes and strange shadows. To them it can be very frightening."

"Well, Cat said she could see the spell and Chuck was freaked out a bit. After I cast, there was a bright flash and the walls, floor, and ceiling were turned to metal. We now live inside a steel box. At least the door opens so we aren't trapped."

Grams began laughing. "That is pretty funny, child! What did you use and who did you call on for your spell?"

"I used some of what the Council teachers have imparted to me. I went old-school and cast a circle first. Then I called upon the Goddess and described what I wanted and visualized the whole thing. I've thought about it and even wrote it down, but I can't see what happened!"

"Who did you call upon?"

"I asked Freya for protection and spoke the words for shield wall."

"That is your problem right there, child! You asked for a shield." She stressed the word shield. "The Goddess took you literally. Especially when you used the words for shield wall. I would suggest that next time you use Athena or one of the other battle goddesses but leave out the word shield somehow. But I am proud of you, Aggy. You changed a building and not an animal this time. It shows you are learning."

"I may have done that too. It's what chased off the last teacher, Montgomery."

"Montgomery? They sent that fuddy-duddy to you? How many teachers have you had?"

"Twelve or thirteen I think. Some of them haven't stayed very long. Montgomery had me doing a diagnostic spell, and I used the wrong word for something and there was a flash. A deer and a rabbit may have been changed into a Jackalope. I don't know how far my spell went this time. I've seen more than one so they might be breeding."

"Don't worry about it, dear. I will notify the Council for you. They should be sending real teachers not the bozo brigade! I will take care of it. Have a good week, Agatha, and call me anytime."

I set the phone down and looked up. Cat was sitting up in bed watching me. "She sounds like a real sweetheart."

"She can be when she wants to be. She really cares about me."

"It sounds like it."

"Did you catch what she said about Weres and magic?"

Cat looked at me and sighed. "I did. Dad's pet wizard told me the same thing, actually."

"You need to decide, Cat. I suspect that our training is going to bring your aspect to light. Hiding in the shadows is not an option anymore."

Cat stood up and walked across the room. She sat down next to me on the bed and gave me a big hug. "I don't want the status change it will cause at home. There can be only one Alpha at a time in the pack. If I try to stay he will challenge me. I don't want to kill my Uncle, Aggy. In that type of pack challenge it's brutal. One wins and one dies. I want to be an FBI agent, not the leader of the pack!"

I rubbed her shoulders. "Vroom vrooom. I have to put that song on your cell phone now. You'd make a good leader, you know that. But I see your point. In my world, rule one is that family is sacred. You don't hurt or attack family. The school doesn't have a designated Pack but you could be an Alpha here. Isn't this considered neutral ground?"

She frowned thoughtfully. "It is. We are allowed to form small packs here. Once we become agents we are allowed to cross pack territories without causing trouble. Mostly."

"How so?"

"Female Alphas are rare. Really rare. I haven't been tested but I'm a lot stronger than many of the ruling Alphas on our Council. Or at least that's what my cat claims. She's really dominant."

"I'm surprised she lets you live with me, then. I know from reading those books you recommended last year that dominant wolves don't like competition."

"They don't. But she says you're a good balance for us. I had no idea you were that powerful, Aggy. You took out three Russian mercs and then the same day, did this!" She waved her hands around.

I looked at her uncomfortably. "I know we had the conversation where I told you I was drafted by the FBI. Right? I mean, not really, but I had very little in the way of choices. Mostly it's my Aunt Camilla's fault. If there was ever someone who deserved to become a pink chicken, it would be her."

"You told me, but I figured some of it was boasting. You had very little time to do any casting last year, Aggy. Those teachers of yours didn't show up until winter break. I've been meaning to ask, did you stay here this Winter?"

"I did, and it really sucked. Winter in Virginia is no fun at all! There are people here, but they're mostly the security guards and maintenance staff. They gave us a big field to use away from everything and then classes for me started. I did learn a few spells and worked on my techniques, but it was a jumble of chaos. None of them followed the same lesson plan or were even on the same page. A couple were pretty funny."

"Did you chase them all off?"

"All but one. There is a troll living under the I-95 bridge. Instead of a toll road it's a Troll road. One of my teachers had me cast a spell to reveal the presence of paranormals. The last time I saw him a large Frost troll was chasing him across the field."

Cat pulled away from me and started laughing.

"They keep sending them and I keep breaking them. After this last one I don't know what will happen. We're not supposed to change living creatures. There are rules."

Cat leaned back in to me and half hugged me. "You are my friend and I love you. I know you won't hurt me. Who cares about the rest of them? Come on, let's go get something to eat in the cafeteria."

We both jumped up and got dressed in a hurry. I checked on Fergus and he was still sleeping. Maybe I would bring him back a treat or something... On our way out of the building we passed a small group of techs working on the camera in the lobby. Hopefully they were removing them.

The cafeteria was like several of the best restaurants you have ever been in all in one place. It had the traditional serving line with various selections, but the food was some of the best I have ever had. They catered to the various races and creeds that filled the halls of the FBI. Weres preferred mostly a high protein diet. The Elves or Fae preferred vegetarian meals. There were supposed to be at least a dozen or so Vampires in the service, but I had yet to see one. They stayed mostly on the West coast. We grabbed a table and hit the line. Loading our trays, we showed our student ID's to the cashier and went back to our table. Chuck was sitting there waiting. He stood and held Cat's chair for her. I gave her a look and a hand motion. She really needed to decide what she was doing with him and soon.

As I ate my breakfast, I looked around the room. The other students seemed to be in a good mood. The unexpected holiday had allowed some of the stress of the first day to dissipate. I perked up when I spotted Director Mills surrounded by Agents and other staffers. They were in one of the private rooms. She looked very tired. I pulled out a notebook and wrote a quick note to her. The message spell is one I learned as a child. Grams and I used to send notes to each other all the time. Using the salt on the table I drew a small circle of protection. I placed the note in the center and concentrated on it. Speaking a single word, I sent the message to the Director.

Academy Director Mills was in a serious conversation with her staffers. The aftermath of yesterday's events had repercussions that were bouncing around like a whole box of rubber balls. Before she could finish her report to her boss, the Director of the FBI, the Witches' Council had been heard from. They were outraged with former Director Offenberg's actions and horrified that the Academy and agency would set themselves up for a battery of lawsuits like that. Then they praised her actions and said she was a credit to the Bureau. Her bosses were as outraged as the Council when she told them what she'd uncovered. Someone must have given Offenberg the go ahead because the money for extra staff and equipment doesn't just grow on trees. The Witches' Council had saved her from the bulk of the fallout, but she still had to clean up her own house first.

"Director, we had authorization to start the program. I swear we did. The former Director showed it to me."

"Well it isn't to be found, now! He's gone and here you are. A large section of your operation is so illegal the repercussions could bring down the Bureau! Fix it. You have less than forty-eight hours before an investigative team from Washington gets here. If they find anything that is not supposed to be here, heads will roll! Don't think I'm ignoring your own personal involvement in this. That student did nothing to deserve the stalking you subjected her to without her knowledge. Your file will reflect that."

She looked at one of the ladies at the table.

"Lisa, how is Human Resources doing? Are you prepared to run the whole staff through race relation training?"

The short blond woman looked up from her notes and responded. "We have classes running this week for the security department. It is going to take the better part of a month to have the entire staff take them."

"Good. Thank you Lisa. Listen all of you! This whole Cluster-frak happened because I wanted to see what a student was talking about. She wondered why she was followed everywhere in the building and everyone she met either drew down on her or reached for their weapons..."

"Ma'am, that witch just about destroyed the school last year! She can't be trusted to roam free!"

"Sub-Director Jonson please turn in your credentials and go home. You're done. Agent Thomlinson?" The large man by the door looked up.

"Take Dick here and escort him back to his office. He is to pack up his personal effects and leave the building. Make sure you collect his badge and creds so he cannot return to the base." She turned back to the former Sub-director. "Pending review of course, you are out of here."

She ignored his protests as he was dragged out the back door. No need for the students to see that. "Now, let's get something straight here about Agatha Blackmore, shall we? The FBI has never had its own Witch before! We use hired hands for our magical needs. I witnessed first-hand the difference between the two. We need her. We need her desperately! The Witches' Council has been trying for years to get a volunteer who would work with us. It was sheer luck that we got her. We need to keep her."

"Director Mills, I don't understand why she's so special. I've worked with the Russians for years and had no problems. They can be very helpful with an investigation. We used the three brothers just last year to take down that wizard in Miami."

"Did they capture him directly or use magic to do it?"

"Well no. They scried him out and put some protection spells on our men. The assault team took him out with special weapons. We only lost two of them in the process."

"Yesterday morning I watched Miss Blackmore take down all three of those same Russian brothers at one time when they attacked her. In addition, she protected the entire field and all the innocents at the same time. According to related information that I have received, the Russians are the minor leagues compared to her and her family. I watched the video from last year. She was the victim. All she did was give her name and over a dozen agents drew on her. When she tried to leave, you opened fire on her. She only attacked when the Marines became involved. Watch it, yourselves if you don't believe me. She told me that if it had been her grandmother instead of her that building and part of the school would not exist anymore. We need her. Get that through your damn thick heads!"

There was a bright flash suddenly that left all those at the table blinking. In front of the Director was a folded note.

"Director, what?!" Director Mills held up her hand to stop any more questions. She carefully picked up the folded sheet of paper and opened it. Smiling, she laid it back down.

"Let's wrap this up, people. We have an investigation to prepare for and classes to start. Any more questions?"

Cat was watching me as I made the note disappear. "What are you doing?"

I pointed to the meeting room and the Director. "She looks too tired. I just told her that."

She shook her head. "Only you, Agatha. Come on, let's go back to the dorm. I have a hard choice to make and I want your help. You were right: I do have to choose."

I smiled at her and picked up my tray. Stepping over to the trash and dish area I began sorting my tray. As I was about to leave one of the security officers cleared his throat. At my glance he spoke. "Miss Blackmore? The Director would like a quick word." He pointed to the kitchen. I looked back at Cat and Chuck and motioned for them to go on out.

The Director was leaning up against one of the kitchen prep tables. She was munching on a carrot. "What's up, doc?"

She smiled at me. "Cute trick with the note! I've never seen that one before."

"Grams taught me that when I was eight. We used to play a game and send each other messages. You look tired Director."

"It's been a long twenty-four hours. Headquarters received a message from the Witches' Council over the incidents yesterday; there was praise for me. I most likely am safe from the witch hunt that will occur. Did you inform them?"

"I told my grandmother this morning, but neither Cat nor I told anyone else. I did destroy the cameras in the dorms. I also did something to our room."

"Is this something I should know about?"

"Sort of? I changed the walls, floor, and ceiling to metal. I was trying to do a shield spell."

She began to laugh. "Sorry; I thought you might have done something a bit more drastic yesterday. Have you given my offer some thought?"

"I'll teach your class for you. It should cover the true history of Paranormals and the US government. I will touch on how magic works and what is both possible and impossible. Some things I have to leave out such as the Council's enforcers or how we punish our own. Everything else the Council should be OK with. Grams said she would clear it with them."

"The Council has enforcers?"

"All the larger Councils do. They keep low profiles, but how else do you think the groups protect mundanes?"

"Then why isn't the FBI working with them instead of hiring Russians?"

I smiled sadly at her. "It all relates to the Purge. They just don't trust you enough yet."

"But it's been almost a hundred years! They don't trust us yet?"

"It's more a case of what happened after-wards explaining 'why' they don't trust you. But I will explain that too if you like. I love history."

"Good! That is what I was counting on. Plan on doing a class two afternoons a week. Your schedule should reflect it. Use whatever free time left over for extra study or lab time."

"Thank you Director Mills. You look so tired. Get some sleep, please?"

"I will. Go ahead and take off. You have a big day tomorrow."

Cat and Chuck were waiting for me near the exit. "So what's going on?"

"Nothing bad, I promise. She wanted to thank me for something I didn't do and ask about me teaching a class on witchcraft to FBI agents."

"Oh, is that all? What didn't you do?"

"Somehow the Witches' Council knew about the whole camera incident. They were pissed! But they praised Director Mills for her quick resolution of the issue. I think they have spies here."

"Ya think? That is a very strong possibility, Aggy..."

As we walked back to the dorm, I watched how Cat and Chuck acted around each other. I had initially thought there was something there, but now it was as if they were siblings not rivals. Something to be said for the whole pack-mentality thing. Whether she liked it or not, Chuck was part of her pack.

The dorm room was just as we left it except for music coming from inside Fergus's home. He was listening to a Katie Berry song and dancing on my desk. All three of us stared mesmerized at him dancing.

"I don't think I will ever sing along to Dark Horse without laughing from now on."

"Thanks Chuck for ruining yet another song for me!" Cat gave him a not-so-light punch to the arm.

We stepped into the room as the music died. Fergus heard us.

"Have a good morning, Ferg? We liked the dancing."

"How much did you see?"

"Only a little bit. You were good!"

He failed to answer and went back into his barn with a mooo. That mooing door made me laugh every time. We sat down on our respective beds and Chuck took a desk chair. "So Cat, why don't you declare as an Alpha?" I asked.

Chuck winced.

"I told you why. It would hurt my family."

I thought for a moment. "Have you asked your family? I bet your dad would be tickled that his daughter was Alpha material."

"That's true... Let me give him a call. He keeps his phone on all the time." She pulled out her cell and entered his number. Chuck was staring at the ceiling. I couldn't remember if she'd told them about him or not.

"Dad? Are you busy? I need to talk to you about something important." I'm not a freaky all-hearing Were that can hear a phone conversation from across the room so I could only guess at what he was saying from Chuck and Cat's faces.

Cat's head was cocked to one side and Chuck started to choke back a laugh. "No. No. Dammit Dad, No! I am not pregnant. Geez! Who has time for that nonsense? No, that is not why I need to talk to you. Stop! Seriously. Is anyone around that can hear this conversation? Can you chase them out? Fine. I can wait." She covered the mouthpiece and shook her head. Both Chuck and I started laughing at her.

He must have started speaking because she put the phone back to her ear. "OK, this is serious Dad. Last year before school let out I was challenged in a dominance fight." She held the phone away from her ear. Even I could hear the "What!"

"Dad. Dad. Dad! It's fine, I won. No. No. It was Charles Winthrop. My roommate calls him Chuck. What? My roommate Agatha. Dad, we talked about this, I know I did. No I'm not imagining it. No. No. Fine! Hold on." Cat held the phone out to me. "He wants to talk to you."

I pointed at myself and asked. "Me? Why me?"

Cat just rolled her eyes and shook the phone. "He can hear you, you know. Just talk to him."

I gingerly took the phone from her. "Hello?"

"Hello, Agatha is it?"

"Yes, Sir?"

"I need to ask you a few questions about my daughter. Is there somewhere you can go that she can't hear me?"

"I can't but hold on, I can fix it so she can't hear." I looked at the two Weres and smiled. I mouthed sorry to them and spoke "þegja" along with a wave of my hand.

"OK, we can talk now. I promise you that neither of them can hear a thing."

"Who else is there with you?"

"Oh, Chuck is here too."

"Does he live there too?"

"No. He just comes over all the time."

"If he's not dating my daughter or has declared her as his mate why is he there all the time?"

"He's her bitch." Cat's dad snorted. I covered the phone and turned toward the two Weres who were now glaring at me. "Sorry, now you know how I feel during these conversations. What? Sorry, I forgot." I giggled. Even I forgot I took away their hearing!

"I just heard what you said to them. How did you do that?"

"I thought Cat told you? I'm a witch."

"Really? I knew the Witches' Council was looking for someone for the FBI, but I didn't know they found someone. What clan are you from?"

"Blackmore Clan. Marcella Blackmore is my grandmother."

There was a lingering silence at the other end of the phone.

"I'm sorry to have questioned you. I've met your grandmother; she is very formidable."

"If that is a polite way of saying she's a Bad-ass then you are right! She raised me from age eight."

"Do you know what Catherine wants to tell me? Is it serious?"

"While I'm familiar with the basics of Were society and Cat has taught me much, I don't know all the details. She really should tell you this. Hold on a minute while I un-zap them." I looked at the two Weres and spoke the word. "Hljóð."

"Can you two hear me now?" They both grabbed their ears and nodded.

"Dammit Agatha don't do that again! You just scared the hell out of me!"

I thrust the phone into her hands. "Talk to your Dad and tell him."

She took the phone. "Dad, I'm an Alpha."

Chapter 6

Robert Moore, Cat's father, actually took the news rather well. His brother Marcus was the pack Alpha, after all, not Robert. Robert agreed with his daughter that she couldn't come home for long visits as a declared Alpha, but she could come home. Marcus would allow short visits if she notified him beforehand and didn't get into any trouble or heaven forbid try to recruit anyone. There were procedures for visiting Alphas. He told Cat he would get with his brother and set up a visitation schedule for her. He said it was a major boost in status for the family to have a rare female Alpha.

Cat had a good cry on my shoulder. She'd really thought she might never see her family ever again. She'd failed to mention to me that the entire time in South Dakota she had been pressuring her cat to not make an appearance. The intentional loss of family was the one curse of any Were. At the first tear I had sent Chuck off and told him we would call if we needed him. It was just us girls and Fergus.

"Cat, honey, it's Ok: you can see your family again. Your father even said it was a great honor to the family to have a female Alpha. What's wrong? You can tell me." I held the small girl in my arms. Her crying had stopped, but I could sense she was still hurting. Empathy was one of the major witch powers and I had a small trace of it. I could sense the major emotions and that coupled with my telepathy gave me a sense of wrongness sometimes. It was one of the things that saved my life last year.

She pulled away from me and looked up at me. "Aggy, thank you for being my friend. I was so afraid I would have to kill Uncle Marcus just to say hello to my mother."

"Didn't they teach you about visitor rules for the pack?"

"Of course they did. But not what to do for visiting Alphas. That just doesn't occur. Sure we can meet on neutral ground or at a pack gathering. But home ground or rather claimed territory is another matter. Most potential challengers don't get twenty feet inside a claimed territory. They kill them before they can hurt anyone. There hasn't been a clan war in over a century. Even during internment the Alpha rules applied. I was so afraid."

"Cat, friends are the family you get to choose. I will always be your friend. I can't speak for Fergus but he might be your friend too."

We both heard him mumbling in his little barn. "Damn sneaky cats!"

I just had to giggle. Fergus was good for comic relief. "Let's get cleaned up. We need to plan for tomorrow. Classes begin!" I checked the time. "It looks like we missed dinner. Want to send Chuck out for Pizza?"

"He'll be happy I'm OK. You were right, Aggy, and I'm sorry I argued. Chuck is pack. I just didn't see it. I hope he's OK with it because I don't think I can give him up, too."

"Give him a call and order some pie's. Tell him to get some sodas too, I think we're out."

Chuck was good with going for food. He was much like Fergus in that he was a movable stomach.

<<<>>>

According to my schedule, I had law enforcement procedures followed by basic martial arts training this morning. After lunch was intro to firearms. I wasn't starting my own class as a teacher until tomorrow. That gave me a day to make up some handouts. Both Cat and I had a hard time waking up. We were up late talking with Chuck about how Packs are put together and how to form a basic one. Ironically, Chuck had been aware that he was in hers.

"Chuck, how did you know?"

"As you might know my father, Charles Winthrop Senior, is the money man behind Volf Advertising. In our family Pack he is a Gamma Shifter. He has never been very dominant in our pack. One of the reasons I'm here is that I am more powerful than he is and he didn't want to see me die in constant dominance battles. I guess I should stop saying our pack when I talk about them... Unlike you, Cat, I really can't go home. I would be challenged within a mile of home, especially now that I smell different."

This puzzled me for a moment. "Chuck, what did you do over the Winter this past year? I mean I stayed here, and I didn't see you."

Chuck shrugged. "I didn't know I wasn't Pack until my father met with me, but I spent it at the beach. Dad didn't really want to head home, so he met me in our family's condo down in Florida at the beach. One sniff was all it took for him to tell me to not come home again. Fortunately, PC beach is neutral territory or my own brothers might have fought me."

"Chuck, I'm so sorry I did that to you! I had no idea I was taking your family away from you!"

"But you didn't. My brothers are assholes! They are enforcers for the Pack and think they know best. I agreed to Dad's idea of being an FBI agent because of the neutrality of the office. I won't be targeted by them or anyone else. My Dad takes everyone to the beach every Winter. I can still see them then. I won't give up this pack for anything!" Chuck clutched his hands in front of him.

I spoke to him gently. "Chuck, I think Cat is afraid you will either leave or take it personally that she forced you into a Pack."

He looked at the both of us. "I checked with human resources when I realized what had happened. The FBI has specific rules for its agents when it comes to Pack membership. Most of the rules are about assignments and getting involved in politics. Pack matters are secondary to the FBI in all things and we are allowed to join them."

"That much I knew. What about Alphas?" Cat looked really anxious.

"They don't have an issue with that. We are supposed to be neutral parties. I know of at least one Alpha Agent. You should be OK. We just have to register our mini-Pack with the administration here on campus but we can call ourselves a Pack. If we let in new members, we should be selective. There are some real losers here."

That much I could agree on, too. Most of the other shifters stayed away from me, but I knew they were here because they had little or no prospects back home. The lure of being neutral was a strong draw.

At least Cat felt better after talking to him. They agreed to a basic format for their small Pack and Chuck took the position of Beta. He was fairly dominant. Both of them told me that no matter what, I was an honorary member of the Pack. So now I'm in a WereCat Pack! I sent Grams a text message, and she laughed at me.

We started the day off right: late and racing to class! Oversleeping just sucks. I hope that law enforcement procedures gets more interesting because the first day was one of the most boring classes I have ever had. Maybe martial arts would be more interesting.

That class was taught in the main gym area. We were all instructed to change to workout clothing or at least loose clothes. Our instructor was a large, well built human. I did a small scan spell that one of the Council teachers had showed me. He was ninety percent human. Ten percent was troll which really surprised me. The how of it had me so distracted I missed his calling my name.

I blinked my eyes a few times as I heard my name being called. "Agatha Blackmore?"

"Here. I mean present." I raised my hand.

"Nice of you to join us, Miss Blackmore. I asked you a question. What martial arts do you already know?"

"Sir, I have trained in Krav Maga." Grams got me a teacher when I was ten. She wanted me to not have to rely on my magic to protect myself until I better understood how magic worked.

"What belt are you?"

"Sir, I'm unofficially ranked Orange."

He peered at me closely. "P two or three?"

"P three" my instructor last tested me two years ago.

"Why did you not compete and are you still in practice?" The whole class was staring at me now.

"I still practice the Kata's daily as part of my workouts. My roommate helps with them as well. I didn't compete as I was both a private student and not associated in any way with the normal community."

"Who is your instructor?"

"Haim Levine from Portland, Maine." Haim was one of Grams oldest friends.

He was nodding. "I know the man. I was unaware that he did private lessons."

"My grandmother obtained his services for me. He owed her."

Thor, our instructor, made a come on motion with his hands. "Who is your grandmother?"

"Marcella Blackmore."

"OK! I can see that. I may use you for class discussions, Miss Blackmore. Be prepared for that."

Thor proceeded to quiz all my classmates on what techniques and practices they had experience with. Out of the class of twenty, over half had some sort of belt in a half-dozen different techniques. The rest were MMA fighters or those with street fighting experience. This was going to be a fun class.

I caught up with Cat and Chuck for lunch in the cafeteria. They had pretty much the same classes as I did except they had martial arts first thing followed by law enforcement. We all had weapons training together and were looking forward to it.

The cafeteria was packed today. It was a shock to see it full of people after months of no one but the staff and I. I grabbed a tray and went through the line. Many of the servers called me by name and knew what I liked before I pointed. I smiled at the cashier and thanked her as I swiped my student card. Chuck was easy to spot as he stuck up higher than most of the other students.

"How was your class?" I sat down next to my friend Cat and smiled across at Chuck.

"Oh. My. God. Is that class boring or what? I thought I was going to fall asleep like twenty times!"

"You did." Chuck had his head down and was eating a massive amount of what looked like Tikka Masala.

"I did? When?" Cat was looking at him with a funny look on her face.

"About halfway, when he started in on local law enforcement rules versus federal. You drifted right off. I caught you just as your head hit the desk. I asked you for a pen remember?"

"I was sleeping? Really?"

Chuck laughed. "Yeah, you were. I figured my Alpha should stay awake for at least the first day of classes."

She turned her head and glared at me. "This is your fault!"

"My fault? How? I'm not the one who ate three whole pizza pies almost by herself!"

"I don't know what you're talking about."

I looked back at her. "Uh huh." I had gotten the vegetarian special, so I concentrated on that.

"Agatha, have you ever fired a gun before?"

I wiped my mouth and thought for a short moment. "Grandmother introduced me to weapons. Cappy, our town sheriff, is sort of useless when it comes to police work. He's mostly for show for the tourists. But he was an Army Captain. According to Grandma he served with distinction in the Dragon Cong War. When the war was over, he returned home not quite right. She said he saw things that scarred him mentally and psychologically. But he does a good job in a town full of witches. He took me out to his range and showed me the basics with a variety of weapons. I'm best with a Colt 1911. Cappy had an original one that belonged to his grandfather. Because he's the local law, he has a few really cool weapons. Somehow he got his hands on a M240 and allowed me to fire it. Ammunition for it is expensive, but I got to fire off a few hundred rounds. Firing that really helped me when it was used against me last year. I have a better spell to defend against that now."

"You told us that story. Do you still have the thingy that caused bullets to bounce off you?" I gave her a sharp look and a slight shake of my head. There were way too many Weres in the room. Besides, I now knew for a fact they recorded this room in security.

"Sorry, Agatha. The reason I asked about the guns is for class today." I nodded. I reached under the table and patted her leg. It was OK, just a slip of the tongue.

"Have you had weapons experience?"

Cat set her third sandwich down and grinned at me. "This Winter in the Dakota's we had contests between the

Packs. I got to target shoot and learned a whole lot about sniper rifles. It was fun!"

"It sounds like it. Chuck, what about you?"

Chuck had finished his meal and was staring at the two of us. "My father doesn't believe in guns, but my brothers showed me the basics when they first became Enforcers. Later as I got older they didn't have time for me so they stopped showing me stuff. I'm a lot rusty. But I have been doing the background reading so I should be OK."

It was sometimes hard to believe that Chuck was smarter than both Cat and I together. His IQ was off the charts. The FBI had wanted him about as much as they wanted me. His biggest problem was he pretended that he wasn't smart at all. Which is why we were surprised when he said things like this. He wanted to be a forensic tech, but I thought he might become a really good investigator. He had a good eye for detail. That gave me an idea.

"Chuck, I have my first Witchcraft 101 class tomorrow afternoon. Can you help me later this afternoon to prepare for it? I need to make up some handouts and get my class notes and visuals ready. If it's OK with Cat?"

Cat reached over and poked me in the arm shaking her head. Chuck smiled at us. "Agatha, I would love to help. Are you going to include information about Weres?"

"I don't know. Your people have been in government service for a long time. Doesn't the FBI know all about Weres by now?"

Cat looked at me and rolled her eyes. "What do you think?"

"I will have to get permission. I don't think the Witches' Council will care but what about the Shifter Council?"

Cat made another face. "I can ask Daddy. They might not care. You and I both know it's all about asking the right or correct questions. The FBI is kind of dumb that way." I heard several smirks from the surrounding tables. Weres; they hear everything.

The official range was way out on the very edge of the Academy's area. It was in the opposite direction from my lab. Fortunately for us there was a shuttle for the class to use. The bus was crowded, over twenty students including the three of us were on it.

"Aggy, where's Fergus?"

"I left him at home this morning. Cat, you know how he gets. His whining gets really old some mornings. I gave him a baggie of salad mix and some root beer before I left. He was happy as a clam. He's probably singing show tunes and acting like he's drunk on beer right about now."

The bus started to slow down, so we all looked out the windows. There wasn't much to see. The range was just a bunch of earth berms surrounded by a really high wooden fence. The building attached to it looked like an old bunker or ammo storage building. I found out later it had been a storage complex for small arms ammunition around the time of the Demon War. It was one of the few buildings left over from that time period.

The insides of the old bunker were as modern as anything else on the base. Our instructor for this class was not an FBI agent. To me he resembled a fire plug. His upper body looked to be all muscle, and he had no visible sign of a neck. I triggered my scan spell, but he was clean, no paranormal genes.

"Welcome to weapons training for the FBI Academy. My name is Command Sergeant Major Finnegan Despertar. This class will introduce you to the weapons you will use for the rest of your life as Agents for the FBI."

He took an abbreviated roll call and dove right into the terminology of what is what when it comes to describing guns and ammo. So many civilians get it wrong. As he described things I made a mental note to send Cappy a note of thanks. The entire time he was teaching me he stressed using the proper names for things. One of the items he'd discussed were the type of weapons we would be using. Current FBI Agents were issued either Glock model 22 or 23's. If we failed to qualify with that particular weapon we would be issued an older Glock 17 or 19. We needed to qualify on one of them to pass the class. Once we reached Probi status, would we actually be issued weapons. These weapons were kept here for students to practice with only. So no gun today. Bummer.

Before class ended, we were given a tour of the facility and given a list of protective clothing needed for shoot days. So far this was my second favorite class outside of martial arts. When we boarded the bus many of us were smiling.

It was several hours before dinner so Chuck drove us over to my lab after I picked up a sleeping Fergus. I knew he would bitch for hours if he missed a trip to the hay factory. We'd all had an excellent day so our mood was high. The ride was uneventful unlike the day before yesterday. We passed several new warning signs that proclaimed it to be a restricted area and to not leave the car. As we approached my lab, I spotted a new fence that now surrounded it and a gate guard. What the hell?

"Chuck, pull up to the guard house. I can't believe this crap." The guardhouse contained two armed Marines.

"This is a restricted area. You need to clear the area." The guard was not smiling. Neither was I.

"Officer, my name is Agatha Blackmore, and that is my lab. I have permission from the FBI to use that building." I held out my badge complete with authorization.

Just like last time the guard took my badge and looked at it. However he didn't draw his weapon. "Ma'am, I can see that; however my orders state that I am to allow no one except military intelligence into that building." He handed me back my things.

"OK, this is bullshit!" I reached into my pocket and pulled out some salt and herbs. I scribbled a note and placed it inside a salt circle. Visualizing who I wanted it to go to I sent it to Director Mills. She needed to call me and tell me what was going on or I was going to start destroying things. Starting with that fence!

CHAPTER 7

Director Mills was sitting at her desk relaxing for the first time in what felt like days. It was just two days ago that her latest nightmare began. Her predecessor certainly left her a big ass mess to clean up. This was the FBI Academy of the federal government; things shouldn't be this screwed up. She did have many good people, and they were taking it all in stride. With any luck, the investigators would leave empty-handed. She knew that was an empty wish, but it was nice to think. She had just closed her eyes for a short nap when she heard a loud "Poof!" come from in front of her. A folded piece of paper was lying on her blotter. Her eyes widened, and she looked around. Agatha didn't say she could send notes without actually seeing the other person. She opened it and groaned. What now?

"Agatha? Slow down. What is happening?" The note had included a phone number and a statement that there was a wall around her lab and she was getting ready to blow it up.

"Director, I'm tired of this bullshit! I came out here to prepare for the class tomorrow and now there is a wall around my lab complete with Marine guards. They won't allow me into my own lab, they say only Military intelligence gets in. I'd like to see them try! Fix it, please. I don't want to declare war on the Marine Corps today!"

"OK Agatha, calm down. Let me call and find out what is going on. Don't zap anyone!" She set her phone down and yelled for her assistant.

"Get General Varmkorv's office on the phone immediately! Did anything come in about Agatha Blackmore's lab out on the edge of the reservation?"

"Nothing about that lab. I would have remembered that. The phone is ringing for the General."

"Base Commander's office how can I help you, Sir or Ma'am?"

"This is FBI Director Mills for the General, please?"

"Ma'am, he is in a meeting and cannot be disturbed. I can take a message and call you back."

"No. This is extremely important and could be very dangerous to the Marine Corps. I need to speak to him right now!"

"OK, Ma'am. I will tell him." The phone switched to anthems and big band music. Delightful.

"This is General Varmkorv! Director Mills what is the meaning of this, I just blew off two US Senators!"

"Why is there a wall around Agatha Blackmore's lab complete with guards? And why are they on FBI property without my authorization?"

"What wall? I know nothing about any wall. It has guards you say?"

"Yes, General. Guards. The Witch in question is being prevented entry by those very same guards who have told her that only Military Intelligence will be allowed inside. General, you and I both know that is impossible. How are they planning on getting inside? We need to fix this. She is preparing to take out the fence. Hopefully just the fence. We need her and the Witches' Council on our side."

"Let me call someone. Damn spooks always causing trouble!" The general clicked off and the damn band music came back on.

She picked up her cell phone and held it up to her other ear. "Agatha? I'm on the phone with the General. I will fix this. Don't destroy anything yet. Please?"

"OK, I will hold off. Ask the General how they thought to get inside?"

On the other phone she heard her name. She dropped the cell and put the office phone to her head. "Yes, General?"

"I checked with them. Damn fools. They assumed that I was taking control of the building and thought to help out. It is my understanding that they are in the wrong. I am issuing orders to allow her into her lab and to shut down the guard station. Do you want the fence removed too?"

"I haven't seen it yet. How about I get back to you on that?"

"That's affirmative. I will notify those gate guards myself it will save time." He hung up on her.

Director Mills picked the cell phone back up. "Agatha, the guards should be receiving a call any minute. Do you want the fence to remain?"

"Sure. Thank you Director."

"We really do need you Agatha. We just don't know how to interact with magic users who are actually on our side."

I hung up the phone and smiled at my two friends in the front seat. "Did you get all that?" Why explain what was going on? They have freaky Were hearing after all.

"Of course we did, girlfriend." They both laughed at my expression. Chuck pointed at the guard shack. The officer inside was at attention and on the phone. We all laughed at the expression on his face as he talked to the General. The guard that was watching us went inside and stood at attention too.

"I think it's about time to go inside." I stuck my head out the window and yelled at the guards. They were off the phone and were packing up all their stuff. "I'm going to my lab now."

I raised my hand and muttered a word. "Skera."

The lock on the gates severed into two pieces and the gates opened all by themselves. "Go ahead Chuck. Make sure you stop just inside the gates." I waved at the guards as we drove through.

The car stopped, and I waved at the gate again. It closed by itself. I turned toward my lab and made a few hand motions and muttered a phrase. Mentally I deactivated one of Grams' presents. "It's safe now Chuck."

"Agatha what happens if someone gets past your defenses and gets inside the lab?"

"I wouldn't want to be them. Grams gave me a few toys that would make life unpleasant for them. Most will get caught in the amber field out here. Speaking of which. Look over there." I pointed to a frozen group of soldiers. They were standing next to a Military Humvee. In their hands was some sort of electronic device.

Chuck stopped the car next to the frozen men. I stepped out of the car and peered at them. Their equipment gave off the glow of being magical in nature. I pried one of the glowing objects out of a Marine's hand. "Chuck, stash this somewhere. I need to look at it later."

Pulling out my phone I called the Director back. "Director Mills? Sorry to bother you again. I have five frozen Marines here. They were trying to get in using some sort of electronic gizmo. Do you want me to hold on to them for you?"

She told me to leave them frozen and to turn them over to a FBI security team.

"Come on Chuck, let's go inside. Cat, can you watch for the security team?"

"Sure. Go on and get the stuff you need for tomorrow. I want to check out their equipment, anyway." We went inside and got to work. I glanced at Cat as we went inside. She was climbing around on the Humvee like a kid at the park.

"Chuck I have a photocopier in my office over there." I pointed to a door on the left. I stepped into the greenhouse and set a sleeping Fergus on his favorite hay field. I poked at him. "Fergus! Wake up."

"It was the horn, I swear! I had no idea she was your wife!" Fergus woke up yelling. He looked around and began jumping up and down. "Hay!"

"Bad dream?"

"I have no idea what you are talking about." He was talking as he ate but I could still understand him.

85

"We are only here for a short while so no hay orgy like last time!"

"Would I do something like that?"

"You bet you would. Cat and Chuck are here with me so behave." He pranced off and began rolling in the fresh green hay. Unicorns.

I stepped into my office and sat at the desk. My laptop had most of what I would need. I quickly put together a handout that gave the basics of what Witchcraft was about and what we could or could not do. For the most part. Grams always told me that everything was possible with the correct spell and meditation. Chuck just laughed at the expression on my face. He had a large handful of paper in his hands already.

"You finished those copies fast!"

"That is a nice machine. It's an old one, but it still works well."

I glanced at the old NCR copier it was older than I was but it did work. "That and the desk were the only things in this place when I got here."

Chuck nodded and cocked his head to one side.

"What's wrong?"

"Cat says the security team is here. They need those guys unfrozen."

"Sure." I dropped into a short trance and waved my hands around. "There, they should wake up now."

"Cat says thanks. She says the security team is freaked out, but they have the marines and their equipment."

"You two freak me out when you do that. Could you do that before?"

"Before we were a pack?"

I nodded yes to him.

"I don't think so. We have really good hearing, but even with Pack bonds some of what we do isn't normal. I will study it and let you know. Thanks Agatha. I needed a new project to work on." I had to shake my head. I was so glad I had met Chuck and Cat.

"Hey do you have that gizmo handy?" Chuck reached into his cargo pants and pulled the shiny controller out. He tossed it to me.

"I will look at this thing another time. For now it goes into the vault." Behind my desk was what looked like a filing cabinet. I said a word, and the illusion faded away. It was a short house safe. Spinning the dial I opened it up and laid it inside. Several lumpy shapes already sat inside. I ignored those for now. The illusion spell was reactivated, and I piled a stack of old files on top of it.

"Forget you saw that."

"Saw what?"

"Exactly. Thanks."

I gathered up all my papers and my small laptop. I might not need it but you never know. I thought for the first class I would just go over the bare basics so I shouldn't need any supplies. I stuck my head into the greenhouse to call to my Unicorn. Fergus was standing in front of my small fish tank talking to them.

"Are they talking back?" The little Unicorn jumped then turned and glared at me. It was his version of giving me the finger.

"No, but I have hopes for them to, one day! Is it time to go?"

"It is." I held out my hand, and he jumped on.

"Why can't we have hay at home? You could grow this in the dorm." I considered for a moment.

"I could... However you would eat so much you'd look like a rubber ball with feet." He didn't answer me as I stuck him in my pocket.

I closed up the lab and mentally tripped the locks. We all climbed into the car and drove to the edge of the parking lot. I mumbled the activation spell and could see in my mind when the defenses triggered. Grams had come up with a very effective system. Her wards plus a self-destruction artifact coupled with a few spells I added in. If the Military couldn't get in I was golden. The Witches' Council could probably breach my defenses, but I had nothing they wanted.

We ate dinner, mostly in silence, at the cafeteria. Cat cuddled up next to me and gave me a big hug. "I finally see what you've been saying. Every time you turn around they are watching you or trying to search out your secrets."

"It's getting a bit better with Director Mills, but yeah." I gazed up at the ceiling for a moment. I could see the small camera looking down at me. I shook my head and made a hand motion. There was a loud pop that had all the Weres looking up suddenly. Small pieces of plastic and circuit boards fell to the floor between the tables. "Sorry." Many of the diners looked in my direction and laughed.

"There are a few problems still. I'm starting to get irritated about my laboratory. I had hoped that by giving the Director that tour I might slow them down a bit."

"Aggy, talk to the Director. She likes you. See if she can do anything."

"She's most likely going to be sitting in on my class so I will. Thanks. Let's get going. I have some law enforcement studying to do before it puts me to sleep." My table mates and half the cafeteria laughed at me.

True to my words I lay in bed later reading the extremely dry and boring textbook. I know that learning this stuff is required but does it have to be so boring? It's definitely the Budge version of Law Enforcement.

The next morning I had the same classes in the morning as the previous day. I was starting to envy those that had martial arts early instead of Law enforcement. I was dragging by the time my martial arts class began. Fortunately it was a day of introductions to different forms. Our instructor Thor had a very interesting audio-visual display for us. A movie would play and he would make comments and show various strikes on a dummy. It was actually very revealing as to what skills we were required to know and to practice. At least I didn't fall asleep in it. Cat and Chuck found me in the cafeteria nose deep in my notes for my history class. While I was intimately familiar with the material, it was always good to review it.

"Hey! Quit stressing out over this class. You know your stuff. It will be fine." Cat sat down next to me and pried the computer from my hands.

"Agatha, you said yourself that you liked history. I seem to remember you telling us this wasn't your first time schooling the FBI about it."

I looked over at Chuck as he sat across from me. "That's true. But I had Grams to help me with it."

"You'll be fine. Won't the Director be there? She will keep the others in line."

I put my hands over my face and sighed. "I guess you're right. They scare me sometimes." I removed my hands and looked up. There were three camera up there now focused down on 'our' table. "Seriously?" I waved my hand and snapped my fingers. Three loud pops came from overhead. This time the Weres barely looked up. I actually heard a few claps.

"That is exactly the attitude you need! Don't screw with the Witch!"

I couldn't help myself and started laughing. How much are cameras like that, anyway? Gathering up my notes I headed back to the dorm. I had about a couple of hours to change and prepare before class time.

Chapter 8

I felt as if my heart was in my throat as I walked to the Administration building. Every time I stepped foot inside I felt as though it might be my last. This place scared me. It bothered me enough to dig out the amulet that Grams gave me last year. It could only be used three times but when activated all projectiles would bounce off me. I had been saving it for when I graduated and became an active agent, but I was worried enough to use it today.

The building loomed ahead of me. I carefully climbed the steps and entered the doors. In front of the reception desk was a sign announcing the class and an arrow. Nodding to the blond behind the desk I followed the signs. No guns were drawn on me yet but I did get some looks. It might have something to do with the box floating behind me. All those flyers and handouts were heavy. When you added my computer it was a bit much. I'm a witch, why not use magic? The signs led me to the large auditorium that I remembered sitting in last year for orientation. Several dozen people were milling around a table set up in front of the doors. A sign in front read Registration. Director Mills spotted me and came over.

"Agatha! Good, you're a bit early. Let me show you how to get down to the stage area."

Stage? "Director, how many people are here for this?"

She wrung her hands in front of her and smiled at me. "When I initially announced the lecture series only a few dozen signed up. But word got out about what happened the other day at your lab and then more wanted to come.

Recent events in the Capital brought in even more. I had to open up the auditorium for your use after that."

I was a bit shocked! There might be hundreds of people in that room. I felt myself start to hyperventilate and forced my body to slow down. "I only brought enough handouts for fifty people. Can someone make me some more?"

"I can have one of the admins take care of that for you. What are you going to discuss?"

Stopping, I reached into my box and pulled out the top sheet of paper and handed it to her. "I thought we should go over the basics. History. The world war and exposure followed by the Demon war. I'm only going to gloss over the major details of that. Much is still a secret both for the military and council. The meat of the issues will be post-war and why the paranormals don't trust governments very much. I can talk about the Russian mercenaries too if you like. I practiced it. Without questions it should take about two hours or so. My computer is with me so I can do a small visual display too."

"This looks really good Agatha. Thank you for doing this. I should warn you, some of the Military will be in there too."

"It's OK. I figured that. Can you do me a favor and tell Security to stop watching my friends and I eat? All those cameras must be getting expensive. I've destroyed at least four so far." The Director made a funny face, and I giggled. "I guess you didn't know."

"No, I did not. Old habits die hard for some people. I will speak to them. Come along, let me show you the podium." We got on an elevator that took us down two floors. It opened up on a hallway with a door at the end. Inside was a small dressing room, bathrooms, and what looked like a kitchenette. "Sometimes our guest lectures go on for a long time."

The kitchenette area had some table space that I used to lay out my papers. I gave a copy of everything to Director Mills and she promised to have enough copies made. The door to the auditorium loomed over to the right. We had peeked through the door before she left. It was filling up.

I ran my fingers through my hair. Could I really do this? I sat on one of the chairs and dropped into a quick meditation to clear my head. As I came out of it I gave the room a hard look. I spotted more of those sneaky cameras on every wall. Someone was determined to watch my every move. I shook my head and made a hand motion. I heard over twenty pops inside the waiting room. Out in the auditorium they could tape all they liked. I felt the need for wards. Even with the reassurances of the Director, I still had a niggling feeling of insecurity.

"Fergus, should I ward the room? I'm still scared of this place." I pulled him out of my pocket and set him on the table.

"Agatha do you think they will try to hurt you again?"

"They might? I just have this feeling that something bad might happen here. I tested poorly for foresight but Grams says I have just a trace of it."

"Something bad is going to happen, and you brought me here?" He started jumping around peering left and right.

"I brought the shield that Grams made for me. You should be fine. So should I do it?"

93

"Anything that protects me is a good thing. Go for it. How about I stay in here while you go out there? Just so I feel safe too."

I shook my head at him while I dug into my pockets for my kit. "Are you sure you don't want to be a pink chicken? You have the chicken part down good."

In my pockets are always several zippered pouches. I like to carry a variety of herbs and other materials with me to use for spells or whatever. I pulled out blessed salt, protection herbs, and a small ankh. The Egyptian Goddess Bast would be appropriate for this venue. She is both a protector and a fighter. I carefully cleared my mind and called upon the four elements to ward and protect this place and me. Using Bast's name I sanctified the room and sealed it with my mental projection. Grandmother told me once that much of what we do could be done without calling upon the ancients and the Gods, but it would not be as effective. Ritual and spiritual gifts are what powered my family's magic. It is what we have believed for centuries. I sprinkled salt and herbs in the four corners of the room. Meditating and saying the names of the Gods I blessed the room and then released the elements. The ward would protect me if attacked and prevent those with ill will from entering; anything else and I would need to deal with it on my own.

I heard a knock at the door and turned. This would be the first real test of the ward. "Come in."

The door to the auditorium opened and Director Mills stepped inside. Behind her were two identical young women and a man I didn't recognize.

"Is it time to start?"

"Almost. I brought the girls for you to meet. This is Beatrice and Betsy. We call them the B's. They work as administrative assistants to me and do much of the unrewarded work around here. They volunteered to pass out your handouts for you."

Smiling at the pretty girls, I showed them the table with what I had brought. They told me more copies were outside the door and ready to be passed out.

"Hey! What about me? I'd like to meet some girls." Both girls were staring at the tiny talking Unicorn.

"Sorry. This is Fergus. He is sort of my familiar. He is a Unicorn that had an accident and ended up small."

I turned toward the Director just as Fergus said. "Hello Ladies!"

Director Mills was talking to the strange man with her. He was unable to enter the room. She was trying to pull him in.

"That won't work."

She turned and stared at me. I was frowning at the man. "Why can't he come inside?"

"I warded the room while you were gone, after I neutralized all the cameras. Only those of ill intent can't enter. He either doesn't like me or intends me some sort of harm."

The Director looked back at the man. "Is this true, Director Lansing? Do you intend to harm Miss Blackmore?"

"That's silly. Why would you take the word of this child?"

"Because I have no reason to distrust her that's why."
She looked back at me. "Agatha this is Director Lansing,
he oversees Intelligence issues for the Pentagon."

"OK. He can enter when he doesn't wish to hurt me. The
wards are a bit specific. Did the cameras in here belong to
him?"

He just glared at me and refused to answer the question.
I telekinetically moved Director Mills and closed the door
in his face. "I will take that as a yes."

"Agatha you can't just do that to someone like him!"

"Sure I can. He wants to hurt me. Should I let him do
that too?"

I made a throwaway gesture. "Don't worry about it. The
Witches' Council is happy with everything so far.
Grandmother says they like you. I'm glad I put up the
ward. I had this little feeling that something wasn't right.
So how soon to start?"

She checked her watch. I found that amusing. Very few
people these days used a wrist watch anymore. "You have
just a few minutes."

I stepped over to the main table and smiled. Fergus had
somehow convinced them to groom him. "Fergus are you
ready?"

"Can I stay in here? Please?" He was playing the whole
big-eyed child routine.

Shaking my head, I said OK. I looked at the girls. "Don't
let him talk you into bringing him treats. He's just playing
you."

Betsy, the one on the right blushed and lowered her head. The other sister just laughed. "She's right, he did play you."

"Don't worry about it. He's had lots of practice over the years. He's a good actor. So, are we ready? All I need for you to do is pass out the handouts to everyone. You can stay if you like or come back here. I'm sure that this is being taped by lots of somebodies." I looked over at the Director. She nodded.

I said goodbye to Fergus and told him to play nice. Opening the door I stepped out onto the stage with Director Mills. The auditorium was full with many standing along the back wall. Holy crapolla!

The Director made the introductions. "Good afternoon everyone. My name is Director Madeline Mills and welcome to the FBI Academy. Many of you passed through these gates already and are making your mark in the world. Today is special. After many years of trying we finally have our first Magical student, Agatha Blackmore. Miss Blackmore has agreed to conduct a special class for Agents of the government so that we may better understand the magical citizens inside our borders."

Saying a quick calming spell to settle myself I touched the gold bracelet on my wrist. It had several gemstones in a pattern. I carefully tapped out a certain pattern and activated Grandmother's protection spell. Feeling safer, I stepped up to the podium.

"Hello. My name is Agatha Blackmore and I am a second year FBI student. I am also a Witch. My family clan is the Blackmore. We live in the great state of Maine." I heard a few claps from the back which made me smile. "My family has lived here since 1607. Our founder was part of the Popham colony. So we have been here as long as this country has been. But, I'm not here to discuss me. Paranormals have existed since the dawn of time. We have always been here. If you look to your mythology or your legends, you can find us. We did a pretty good job of hiding too. The Witch hunts of the middle ages and those here in Salem drove many of my kind underground. We, like the vampires, stayed off the radar of the mundanes. Were folk have no magic or strange diets so they blend in better. The world modernized, and we were lost in the shuffle. Until what you like to call the World War." I took a sip of water and looked around the room. I motioned to the twins to start passing out the handouts.

"The B's are passing out a few pages of notes and information. The timeline is one that most paranormals already know. The rest I will get to. In 1914, war broke out in Europe. The governments of the world rushed to battle each other. Paranormals for the most part stayed far away from it except in Germany and Austria. Every race has a bad egg or three. We all have those that refuse to toe the line and work toward the future. The Witches of Fleisch und Blut were our bad eggs. They wanted war, and they wanted power. What they wanted was control of a country and of an army. They coerced the Vampires to help them by using forbidden spells on them. The Vampires then attacked the allied troops at night devastating them. How do you kill something that is already dead? The Witches used magic to control the skies by enchanting German planes and bringing forth Dragons from the netherrealms. Since the cat was out of the bag, so to speak, English paranormals then revealed themselves to governmental authorities and volunteered to help. Now here is where your history and our history diverge and don't say the same things." I stopped and glanced at the Director. Her head was down studying my handout.

"The allied governments, once they got over their shock, begged us to do something about the Vampires. We tried to explain about the Witches but were ignored. All they wanted was a solution to the Vampire problem. Let me mention Vampires briefly. I only know what all paranormals know about them. If you want detailed information you'd have to ask their council. But they are normally a peaceful people. They only take new candidates from those that are terminally ill or have had very bad accidents. The British Council decided to create a great spell. Other councils around the world warned them of the consequences and problems that could arise but they pushed forward, anyway; they wanted to help their government. The leader of the London Vampire Coven volunteered to be a part of the spell. The goal of the Magickal folk of Britain was to separate the two races and shield the innocent Vampires from the Fleisch und Blut Witches. No deaths were intended at all. That was not the point. So the spell was triggered and something unexpected happened: the vampires died."

"The paranormal races call the World War 'The Purge'. The Vampires that were being used to attack allied soldiers died along with every vampire in a 5000 mile radius surrounding Paris, France. The Generals and the Allied leaders were ecstatic and patted each other on the back. The British Council was devastated. Imagine a modern city such as Washington or Miami. Now kill every single soul that lives inside. That is the amount of people that the spell killed. Not a few hundred, not a few thousand, but tens of thousands, hundreds of thousands, we really have no exact number. The Vampire Councils could have told us, but they were all gone. To us it was one of the greatest atrocities of the last century." I looked out at the crowd and could see a visible reaction. Even the Director sat there in shock.

"Many of you are wondering why this is not in the history books? We did tell your governments what had happened. But they had a war to win and didn't care about a bunch of blood suckers. But we did. The only vampires to survive were those that lived on the far Western coasts of North America and those in Japan and parts of China. The Germanic Witches of Flesh and Blood were also wiped out completely. Not by your armies. We suspect it was by vampires but even they deny doing it. The British Witches' Council were put on trial on charges of genocide by a council made up of elders from all the races. Those directly responsible for creating the spell were punished. They were not killed but what happened to them is not written down it was so bad. As you see on my handout that was the first reason for our alienation with your governments and our subsequent lack of cooperation."

I took a few breaths and calmed myself again. "I'll take a couple of questions and then we can break for a bit so you can use the bathroom or eat something." I looked up at the audience.

"How could a worldwide trial happen and nobody know about it?" The man asking was wearing a three-piece suit, so I guessed not an agent.

"That is easy. Through the use of magic and the telegraph. Radio was in its infancy at that point. But signals could be sent and received. By the war's end no one in Europe wanted to hear about Vampires anymore. There were other issues."

"How do we know you are telling us the truth?" That was from the Director that didn't like me.

"You can ask any of the local councils. They will confirm it. Ask any paranormal. We are all taught this in school so that it won't ever happen again. Many will need permission to talk to you but they can easily get it. Most of this is not a secret."

"I will finish the second part in twenty minutes, thank you." I turned and went back into the lounge area. There I found the B's feeding Fergus carrots. All I could do was shake my head.

There was a knock and Director Mills came through the door. That other Director tried to follow and was stopped again by the ward.

"Agatha that was incredible! Is what you said really true? Did that many Vampires really die?"

"It was probably more than that. There is a reason why they dislike Europe and the East coast. I have not met any Vampires but my Grandmother knows several. History is written by the victors. No one wanted to admit they almost killed off an entire race of people."

I watched the girls giggle as Fergus trotted around putting on a show. He might be a Unicorn but he was all ham for the ladies. "My plan with this class is to finish the history tonight and then later this week do the Witchcraft portion."

"Yes, I think what you have said so far is earth-shattering enough for one day."

"That was my thought too. I'm actually glad you asked me to do this. I love history, it's one of my passions. The Council was very happy about this too. Or at least that is what Grams texted me. They want the real history to get out."

"I think this may make you a few enemies, Agatha. Many in Washington don't want closer relations with the Para's."

I gave her the look that Grams saves for me. "Do you think we don't know that? The Council has spies everywhere. I will be fine. I think it's time to piss off some more people. Let's get back out there."

This time I went first and strode right out onto the stage. The room was full again as many wanted to hear the rest of it.

I launched right in. "Now - as a radio host used to say - for the rest of the story. After the war, governments didn't know what to do about Paranormals. The public was scared of us and many governments did nothing to alleviate that. The Weres were easy targets and submitted to being herded onto reservations and kept under guard. The surviving Vampires hid themselves away again. The Fey disappeared into their forests and glens, and the Witches? We kept very low profiles. Much of that didn't matter. Small towns being what they are exposed many a Para. Some few ran to what they perceived was the safety of the government to protect them. It was like painting a target on their backs. Hundreds were lynched, burned, and hunted down. It was a second dark age for us. No government agency wanted to go on record as helping us. So we hid, and we waited. Then you came to us. Someone in Germany had let loose a Demon Prince and Evil was loose again."

"What did we say when you came to us? We said NO. You will not find that in your history books either. Over in Europe the paranormals were asked the same thing. They wanted to say no too, but they were known and many governments took their children into protective custody. They had no choice but to help. The Weres took a chance and refused as well. They were already locked up what more could be done to them? The paranormals here in the United States decided to change their minds and cut a deal. The Council would lend some of it's Enforcers to the War effort. In exchange they wanted certain concessions. We made sure that the US government stuck to it. We would help, but the cold war would end. The Weres would be set free and many would fight for you. The Magical people would help put the genie back in the bottle in Europe. We did as you asked and when many governments tried to weasel their way out of the deal, we publicized it. Radio, television, news media, everything we could think of to say and show how paranormals helped to win the Demon War. But still there were issues and problems. Postwar magic users were still ostracized and run out of town. We once again asked the government for help and were denied. We could not trust you to live up to your promises."

"Other than the Weres - who have always been the most integrated with human society - and a few of the others, no magical people have helped any government officially since the 1940's. The Slavic or Russian mercenaries don't really count. The Russian Volkhvy - what they call their priests and priestesses - ruled the magical clans of Russia with iron fists. It was they that kept the Russian Czar in power and denied it to the Bolsheviks. The Demon threatened them the most. It was they who cast the spells that kept it busy and trapped in Berlin for the Allied armies to even get close enough to use their weapon of mass destruction. The explosion and the aftermath of the spell they'd cast burned them all out. They were only effective if they combined power and they sacrificed themselves to accomplish it. The power vacuum they left allowed the Bolsheviks to rise to power and touched off the revolution inside Russia. None of the lesser magicians had the training or the power to revive the priesthood. Even if the new Soviets would allow it to happen. They hire themselves out now to bring money home. The government actually encourages them to do so. As a Magical community they are a shadow of their former selves. In a couple of days I will talk about part two: Witchcraft and what it can and can't do. I hope to see you then."

"You won't be seeing anyone because you are under arrest!" The creepy Director was standing in front of me holding a gun.

CHAPTER 9

"Arrested for what?" I just stared at the gun pointed at me.

"Sedition, lies, or something like that. I don't need a real reason."

"I may be new to the whole FBI thing, but I think you do need a real charge seeing how you are doing this in a room full of Government Agents." I pointed to the people in the audience.

"They don't matter. Everyone here works for me in some capacity. Now: off the stage, you are coming with me."

"Sorry but some of those police procedures actually sunk in as boring as that class is and you are doing it wrong. I'd like to see a warrant, badge, or even a reason for arresting me. Right now you are the one breaking the law."

I could see a small group of FBI security making their way around the stage out of the corner of my eye. I had a spell I could use, but I was afraid to use it. What if it went wrong?

The creepy Director laughed. "The law? Just who makes those laws? This is your last chance. Off the stage or I shoot."

Screw it. I started to make a hand motion just as he fired. Blam! His gun went off, and the bullet ricocheted off my shield and hit the video screen to my rear.

He just stared at the gun in his hand and pointed it at me and fired again. The second bullet bounced off my shield and went zinging into the crowd. He was about to fire again when he was tackled by the security team. They had him down on the ground and in cuffs in the blink of an eye. Director Mills approached me and escorted me back to the preparation rooms.

"Agatha, are you OK?"

I nodded. "I'm fine. My shield stopped his bullets. I had a dream? Or something that told me that bad things might happen today. It's why I was so scared of even coming inside today."

"You knew this might happen?"

"Not really, Director."

"Madeleine, please. At least when we are alone."

Smiling wanly I sat down on one of the very comfortable couches. "Foresight is a very rare and sought-after Magical power. As children we are tested for a wide variety of the powers. It guides the training we receive. I tested positive for Foresight but only just. I have an extremely tiny trace amount of the power. When it combines with my other powers, it can make me shoot more true or make better guesses. I can't control it or define what it tells me directly. I just had a very uneasy feeling about this building today. Nothing concrete in the least."

Madeleine nodded her head slowly. "Is that why you allowed the Unicorn to stay back here?"

"Some. Fergus can be a distraction for some people if they are not prepared for him. I intended to show him to the audience during my next lecture as a lesson for what can happen if uncontrolled magic is used."

Boom! Boom! Boom! We both jumped. Someone was pounding on the stage door. Madeleine jumped up and stepped over to the door. She stepped to one side and opened it.

"Yes?"

"Director Mills?"

"Yes? And you are?"

"FBI Internal Security. We need you and the Witch to come with us."

"Under whose authority? I'm the Director here. She is one of my students."

"Ma'am, this comes straight from the top."

I was watching the 'Security' and his associates. None of them made any movement toward the door or attempted to push past the Director. "Madeleine. Invite them inside."

She turned and looked at me. I made both a swirling, and a come here motion with my hands.

She nodded to me and turned back to the supposed Security officer. "Step inside and we will discuss it, please." Madeleine stepped back from the door. The Officer started to step forward and stopped like he hit an invisible wall.

"Who are you and who sent you?" She had her cell phone out, she took his picture and was calling the security detail.

The man cursed and kicked at my ward. "You haven't heard the last of this!" He and his associates stormed off and disappeared into the milling crowd of Agents. The real security showed up seconds later and were able to step inside the room.

"You called for us, Ma'am?" The Director looked at me and shook her head.

"Yes, is the area secured? I would like for Miss Blackmore to be able to return to her dorm in peace."

"The assailant is under arrest and he is being transported to a holding cell downtown. We still need to finish taking statements including yours and hers. But as far as we can tell he was alone. Do you know who he was?"

"Yes, he is Director Lansing. He works out of the Pentagon. You should call the transport group and request they call in more backup. He may try to escape." She pulled the man aside and explained about the men that came to the door. She showed her cell pictures as proof.

I stood up and walked across the room to talk to Fergus. He was still in the company of the B's. They were subdued and very quiet. "Fergus, you don't look well?"

"Did someone try to kill you, Agatha?"

"They did. But as you can see I'm unhurt. How about you? Have the B's kept you entertained?"

"Are you sure you are alright? They aren't coming in here are they? I'm not one of those sneaky cats! I only have one life, not nine. Is there a place for me to hide?"

"Fergus, they are not after you. You are perfectly safe." I looked at the two pretty girls sitting in the corner. "Are you OK? It was a lone shooter and they have him in custody. Has Fergus been a pain?"

"Oh, he's been great. He told us a story about field mice and purple squirrels. Did you really turn all of them in town Purple?"

"I did. I was four so I don't really remember doing it. Was he the hero of the field mice story? Because he's scared of them. They think he's a God or something and try to worship him. Don't let him kid you. They really freak him out."

The two cute blondes were not as quiet now and began to tease Fergus. I stepped back over to the officers just as the Director turned to me.

"Agatha can you give a statement to the security officers? They just need to know anything you can remember."

"Of course, Director. Don't forget about the cameras out there, too. Especially those other ones. They are in here too but they weren't working at the time."

They sent men to track them down and trace the signals. The cameras in here were all little molten balls of plastic.

"Director, may I send a text to my roommate and tell her I'm OK? She will be worried." The Director remembered Cat and told me it was OK. I sat down at one of the tables and sent a quick text.

"Ready when you are, Officer."

The interrogation took over an hour. They asked me the same questions over a dozen times. Each phrased differently to try to trip me up. Finally the Director had to step in. "You do realize that she is an FBI student, and she is aware of interrogation techniques? I think you have enough. She is available here on campus any time you might need her."

The security men pried several of the melted cameras from the walls and stepped out of the room. "Sorry about the cameras. I thought they were yours."

"It's OK. I do understand. I was able to watch the footage from last year. Our Agents did open fire first. You shouldn't have tried to walk away, but they seriously underestimated you. Do you have any clue why these people want you?"

"I have no idea. Maybe they don't want the truth to leak out about paranormal relations? Almost every Para has the same info that I do. I just have permission to speak about it. I'm sure somebody will figure it out. Can I go home now?"

"Sure. I will escort you. You better get your Unicorn. The B's will have him on their work desks before you know it. They love small creatures. Especially the cute ones."

"I could use a few new Unicorn sitters. He can be real trouble sometimes." I scooped up the troublemaker in question and placed him in my pocket.

"Thanks girls! Anytime you want to play with him give me a yell." They both smiled at me.

We were on government property so there was no news media or helicopters. That was a no-go on a Marine base. I suspected they would cover the whole thing up. While it was a short walk to the dorm, they gave me a security escort. I thanked them and entered the dorm.

"There she is!" I looked up at the room full of Weres and other paranormal students.

"Agatha, are you alright?"

I smiled at Cat. "I'm fine. No new holes."

"What happened? We heard there were shots fired and that the campus was in lockdown. Even the base was on alert."

I waved everyone into the TV room. The TV was centered on the wall and instead of chairs there was this large tiered wooden structure covered in carpet. It was multifunction so there was room for everyone.

"I gave the first part of my lecture about the true history of the Purge and relations afterward. A government employee pulled a gun, told me I was under arrest and shot at me. Twice." I proceeded to tell them about his arrest and my statements to security.

"Did they arrest him?" this came from one of the first-year students.

"Of course they did. Remember where you are. This is the FBI. Now I'm safe and so are you. If something threatens any of you, I will help to defend this dorm and others. Para's help each other, remember? Thanks for worrying, guys." Being the only witch on campus was both a good and bad thing. The others tended to follow my lead in many things.

Cat and Chuck gave me a big hug. "We were so worried for you, Aggy!"

I tapped my wrist where they could see and tossed my head in the direction of the stairs. We quickly went upstairs and into our room. Once inside I relaxed for the first time in hours. I sagged against the closed door and sighed. "Thanks guys. This has been a hell of a long day so far."

Plopping down on my bed I laid down flat and stared up at the ceiling. I spoke my suspicions bluntly. "Someone or something wants me dead or out of commission."

"What? Agatha what are you talking about?" I explained about the mysterious Director and the fake security guards.

"But he's under arrest right?"

"He is but I will bet you a pizza that he either escapes or is let go by the government. Someone doesn't want me to explain things. It can't be the Council. They could have just said no to the class in the first place. It has to be a government entity. We need to be more careful from now on."

"Is there anything you can do?" I had to think on that. I didn't know the bullet bounce spell. Grams refused to teach it to me.

"I can ward Chuck's car so no one will mess with it or bug it. This room is already taken care of. Chuck, do you want me to ward your room too?"

The big Were cocked his head to one side and thought about it for a moment. He was more analytical than we were. "I don't think so at this time. My roommate would freak I think. He's not wound real tight, but he's a nice guy. I don't want to scare him. If bad things happen, I will just crash here." Cat nodded that that was OK with her.

"OK. That is your choice and I respect it. I'm going to make up a few protection amulets and you will wear them. Understood? Both of you will get one." They both nodded.

Cat came over and sat down on my bed. I sat up and gave her a big hug. "I was fine; I wore Grandmother's bracelet. For once my foresight gave me a clear sign. I was very nervous inside that building. One good thing that came of it: the Director asked me to call her by her given name. She has become a friend to me at least. She is a good resource for us." I pointed to the three of us. If we were going to be a Pack we needed to act like one. "That reminds me. I'm a Witch in a Shifter pack. Is there some way for me to feel the pack bond?"

"I... have no idea? I guess I can ask Daddy. What do you think, Chuck?"

He made a funny face by scrunching his up. "I've read some of the pack histories. Many of the packs are diverse. My father's has cats, wolves, and even a couple of the rare ones like snake shifters in it. Most of the wolves prefer wild, wide-open spaces which is why so few of them are in the service. I have heard that the Alaska packs have allowed other para's to come under their umbrellas of protection, but not inside the actual pack. I can research it some if you like?"

"Why don't you do that. I will email Grams and ask her. She might know a way to connect us together. It would really help if one of you were in danger." They both agreed that was a good idea.

Chuck went back to his room: he wanted to study. The restlessness was making me crazy, so I pulled out some of my supplies and my sewing kit. Most of what I needed for the protection bands I envisioned was here in my room. I only needed a couple of things from my lab and hair from Cat and Chuck to make it work.

Finally, too tired to work anymore, I crawled into bed. My dreams were filled with panic and terror. Small child-like screams echoed through my brain. I woke with a splitting headache and more questions than answers. My foresight was raising its ugly little head again. I would need to call Grams and tell her. All active foresight users needed to be reported to the Council.

My classes were very subdued for the rest of the week. I was informed that the man that shot at me disappeared from police lockup before he could be identified or interrogated. All evidence including the video images vanished as well. My second Witchcraft class was moved to the following week. I was thankful for that. I think we all needed a weekend to relax and cool off.

My dreams were getting worse each night. I wondered if they were coming to me because of the mystery man or something else. Grandmother informed me that her mother had been one of the most powerful seers in her generation. Even though my potential for constructive use was very low, she thought I might be receiving something. She told me to check with the Director. Maybe there was something happening locally that was causing it. She said nothing was in the National news. One bright piece of news though was she knew of a way for me to tap into the Pack magic. Grams said she would research it further and send it to me.

Monday mornings Police Procedures class was actually interesting for a change. It was on arresting procedures and practice. I thought back to the events of the previous week and could pick out what was done incorrectly and what was right. Many of my favorite TV crime shows were nothing but fantasy from what our instructor just taught us. Maybe it wasn't so boring after all.

I showed up for Martial Arts class dressed out but was told to go to the Administration building. The Director wanted to see me. I quickly redressed into my uniform and hustled to the main building. Unlike the previous week it didn't give me that feeling of dread. The same mousy blonde was still behind the desk. She must have a cot or something back there.

"You again?"

"Yes? I was told the Director wants me."

"She does. There are visitors from Washington with her so don't start a war." She pointed down the hall. "Go on."

That was more words than she had spoken to me at one time since I first walked through the doors over a year ago. Briskly walking, I hurried to the Director's office. Four very large and obviously Russian bodyguards stood in the middle of the room. They looked me up and down as I entered the room and dismissed me as no threat. I glanced at the new secretary. The old one didn't pass the new HR tests. "The Director sent for me?"

The harried looking secretary glanced at me and perked up immediately. "Miss Blackmore! She has been waiting for you. Let me tell her." He picked up the desk phone and called a number.

"Director? Miss Blackmore is here. Yes, Ma'am. I will send her right in."

He looked at me and smiled. "Good luck. I think you know the way."

I stepped over to the door, knocked and then opened it. Madeleine was at her desk. In front of her were two men in suits and a police Captain.

"Ma'am, you called for me?"

"Agatha, thank you for coming. Have a seat please." I sat in the chair next to her desk, facing toward the three men.

"This is her? She's a kid! How is she supposed to help us find them? Director I protest. We need to be doing something, not playing with toys."

"Senator Payne, calm down. I said she could help, and I meant it." She looked over at me and smiled.

"Agatha. This is Senator Payne from Georgia and Senator Owen from Massachusetts. The Captain is from the DC police. They are here to see if you can help them."

"Help them how?"

The police Captain was the goat. He baited the trap for them. "Over a week ago there was a couple of high profile kidnappings in the DC area. Two children were taken from the homes of a Senator and the Mayor of Alexandria. Two days ago these two gentlemen's children also disappeared. We involved the FBI soon after."

I looked toward the Director. "Because of the nature of the case the media hasn't been told. They know something is going on but secrecy has held for now. The bureau has committed all of our resources to this. Including you. Can you help us?"

"Of course I can. What has been done so far?"

"Standard procedural forensics and they brought in several of the Russian teams."

I groaned and rubbed my forehead. "They should have called me earlier. Those idiots will only mess up the crime scenes and blur the evidence."

"Agatha, it's political. The Witches' Council hasn't made any friends lately."

I shook my head. "Once again, you don't understand. It's children. If you had told them, they would have helped. We do not sacrifice innocents. Ever."

"Just who in the hell do you think you are, girly? I paid good money for some of those Russians! They do good work."

I looked at the Senator from Georgia. "What do you pay them to do? What does the contract say?"

"I pay them to protect my house and act as bodyguards for me when I'm out in public."

So stupid. "Then that is what they do for you. Exactly that. They protect your house. Not what is inside but the house itself? If you ask them directly I will bet they allowed the kidnappers to enter as long as they didn't harm the house. That is the problem with Mercenaries. They are very literal."

"The hell you say!" The Senator jumped up and stepped out of the office. I followed along with the others. This should be fun.

"Sergie, what do I pay you for?"

The large Russian looked down at the pudgy man from the peach state. "I protect the house and you when you are in public."

"Did you let the kidnappers just break in and take my little Marcie?"

"Nyet. They didn't break in. We protect for that. The house was not harmed."

"I asked you to run scans and try to find my daughter! DId you even do that? You said you did!"

"Senator we did as you asked in the contract you had us sign. We ran the scans, but need a new contract to share the information. It is rules."

"How much to tell the Senator what happened to his child?" I hated to interrupt, but I wanted to know.

The four bodyguards reacted at the same time. They had forgotten I was in the room. "Is small thing. Say five hundred American dollars. Up front."

"OK, Senator, I know you must have some money on you. Cough it up. We need five hundred dollars to give the Russian man you hired."

The money appeared and was given to the merc.

"Give."

"Of course. Girl was taken through wards at weakest point, the roof. She was bound in zmeya charm and smuggled into a van. Van drove through gates and reengaged protections."

"You just let them?"

"Of course. House protected. Is what money is for? No?"

CHAPTER 10

To say my meeting with the Director was traumatic was an understatement. The two Senators sat in shock back in her office. They could barely speak. The four Russian mercenary bodyguards still stood in the outer office. They didn't understand why their primaries were so upset. To them a contract was a contract was a contract. You did the terms of the contract, nothing more. They were not paid to think outside of their set contract limits.

"Why is it when you get involved that things get so out of hand?"

"Director I can leave if you like. I just told the truth. I can't believe that you people didn't already know this stuff. What is the definition of Mercenary to you? To those four out there thinking outside the box is never an option. Why do something without a tangible reward?" I pointed toward the doors. We were back in Madeline's office sitting at the desk.

She shook her head. "I think as law enforcement: that if you are hired for a job, you do that job. We can't imagine allowing a perp inside the house to kidnap someone and then letting him go and not doing anything. As long as the house was undamaged they wouldn't act. It boggles our minds." The Director looked very upset.

"From their point of view they did the exact job. Remember, they don't have a leader anymore. Not one that they recognize. They only take orders from themselves or whatever the contract says. Ask any Russian businessman and they will tell you the same thing I just did. Do you still want my help?"

She looked at the two Senators. "Well gentlemen? Do you want the FBI's help or not?"

"It can't hurt. I don't understand what is happening here." The Senator from Massachusetts looked distraught.

"I need to speak to their Russians and to the FBI's as well. Ma'am, I don't know all the procedures yet. What if I screw up?" We were both standing and walking out to where the Russians were.

"Agatha, don't worry about procedure for now. I think with you being involved that may go right out the window from now on. Besides, those are United States Senators in there. I think you are covered."

The four mercenaries were now sitting in the chairs watching the door as we came out. I stood in front of them and asked. "Privet vy govorite po-angliyski?"

"Yes, we speak English. We understand much."

"Good. Khorosho. When the girls were taken what did you see? I know that you only did your jobs. But what else did you see?"

"Why? You no pay for service. We owe you nothing." He turned to the others and remarked "Sumasshedshaya devushka. Net platit' ne rabotayut." The other three men all laughed.

"What did he say?"

"Just that I'm crazy." I looked back at the men. Time to play my hole card.

I made a small motion with my hand and then addressed the ringleader. "Still no answers? How about I turn the lot of you over to the Witches' Council for breaking contracts and causing problems?"

"You aren't Council. We don't have to listen to you." He looked over at the others, they were frozen to their chairs. All that could move was their heads.

"Ivanov? Vasiliev?" He peered at the man on his left and poked his arm. Grabbing the man he gave him a shake. "Alexeev, wake up! Vstavat' len'. Chto ne tak s toboy?" Alexeev's eyes were wide open and his mouth moved but no sound escaped.

The speaker jumped up and towered over me. "What you do?" He raised his hands as if to hurt me and I zapped him as well. He fell as if poleaxed onto the floor. With a wave I unfroze the group.

"Now. Is someone ready to help me? Or would you like to be statues from now on? Statui navsegda!"

Once they recovered from being frozen they all four spilled what they either saw or could trace in the houses.

"How long have you spoken Russian?" Madeleine was staring at me as I watched the more trained FBI investigators interrogate the Russians.

I looked over at her. "Grandmother wanted me to know things. Russian, German, and Old Norse are the three languages I can speak fluently. I know and understand some elvish, troll, and selkie and can write in Sanskrit. When my mother had her... episode and couldn't handle living in the real world anymore Grams took me in. She hired tutors and home-schooled me. None of the local mundane or Witch schools would take me. My family saw to that. They were scared of some of the things I could do. Most Witch children can't do some of the large magics. It

121

takes many years of study to get to where I am today." I looked up at the ceiling and waved my hand. There was a series of loud pops. The Director glanced upwards as well. "Between you, me and the walls she has been training me to one day be her possible successor. Don't worry, she has a great many years before we get to that part of our story."

"The budget numbers from security are going to be astronomical this year aren't they?"

"I'm guessing even you didn't know about those cameras?" She nodded at me and I laughed.

"So what's the plan, Director? I will need to see the crime scenes to trace the magic. I've only done a diagnostic a few times. The Council's teacher was a little inconsistent but I think I know what I did wrong the last time."

"You realize that doesn't reassure me? Right?"

I just smiled and shrugged my shoulders.

"I will notify my boss that you are willing to help. I can't leave the school but I have requested that one of my old partners assist you. Trust me, you'll like her."

"Is she a good agent?"

"She is. Her name is Tayanita Lowrey. She prefers to be called Nita."

"How come you aren't still a field agent?"

"I wanted a life with my husband and my daughter was growing up. I really didn't want to miss being with her. I stepped down and took an administrative position. When this came open I took it."

"Well I'm glad you're here and not piss boy."

She started laughing. "Please don't call him that."

I just smiled at her.

"He has a name."

"It's more fun this way. When does your partner get here?"

"She doesn't. We have to meet her in Washington."

"Why are we still here then?"

"Well, I had to request transportation and you need to go pack for at least three days. Bring anything you will need, magical or otherwise. So go pack all your supplies."

I practically ran back to the dorm. Running through my head were all the things that I might need for spell work. I ran up the main stairs and burst into the room. I was digging through my closet when Cat came in looking for me.

"Hey! We missed you at lunch. Why didn't you answer your phone?" I immediately patted my pockets and remembered that I left it sitting on the Director's desk.

"Oops! I left it in Director Mills' office. I was in too big a hurry to notice."

"OK, spill!"

"Fine. There have been a series of kidnappings in Washington. They want me to help." I filled her in on what the Russians had done. Or not done as was more the case. I had all my clothes packed; now I was just staring at my supplies. I was going to have to hit the lab before leaving.

"That's crazy! They just let them take those kids and didn't stop them?"

"Nope. Remember what I said about using Merc's?"

"That you did so at your own risk?"

"That. And that they really can't be trusted. Money is all they value now that they have no honor anymore."

"Is Chuck available to run me out to the Lab? I'm going to need stuff. Want to come along?"

Cat looked at me funny. "To Washington or to the Lab?"

"If you want to come along, I can ask. What's the worst she can say?"

She nodded eagerly.

"Can I borrow your cell phone?"

I called the Director while Cat tracked Chuck down.

I thought I pleaded my case rather well. Cat could be useful: she was pretty dominant and most shifters wouldn't give her any crap about anything. She was familiar with me and could carry much of my equipment. Powerful does not mean strong. I can carry one bag not four. Madeleine Mills didn't say anything until I finished talking. She laughed at me and told me that it was OK and she had been going to suggest I take either Cat or Chuck as protection. I also asked if she would bring me my cell phone. I really need to put a retrieval spell on that phone since I keep forgetting it.

I loaded Cat down with stuff. These were high profile kidnappings so I would need to bring my 'A' game and kick ass. It wasn't just herbs I had in lab. Witches use everything from nature in our spells. Many of the world's best magical artifacts are made from something natural. Grandmother taught me well in how to protect and defend myself magically. The dreams I had been having just had to have something to do with the kidnappings. In all of them I'm running or someone is chasing me. Buried in the far back of my stores are my offensive weapons. I was stockpiling these for the days I was on my own or had an active mission. It took me almost an hour to dig out three iron-bound boxes from the pile. They were on the very bottom.

Grandmother had been very specific about what was in the three boxes. They were part of the reason for the extra heavy defenses on this place. Most Witches knew at least one or two defensive spells and many more offensive ones. You cannot survive out in the world without them. My family was no different. We were known for our battle magic techniques. Or at least grandmother is. Battle magic uses a lot of personal energy. So we cheat sometimes and use magical hand grenades. It takes over half a year to make them and a lot of resources. That is one of the many projects I worked on in my lab. This batch I made last year and stashed with the few that she had sent along as models. They completely filled the first two boxes. The last one was special, and I had to think very hard about whether to take it.

"What are those?" Cat was watching as I loaded a special vest with the grenades.

"Magical hand grenades." I kept placing them in the pockets.

"What did you say they were?" Her eyes were very large.

"They're grenades, but magical not explosive. They cannot be used by mundanes or non-magical folk. My family is famous for them."

"Why are you bringing them?"

"Sometimes power is not enough? Or at least that is what Grams drummed into me. Better to have them and not need them than not have them and need them desperately. I like to be prepared." I laid the vest on the top of my packed clothing. "Let's get back to the dorm and get your stuff."

Chuck was waiting for us along with Fergus. "I wish I could go with you."

"I was actually given a choice by the Director: you or Cat. I chose Cat. There will be a next time. Your time will come don't worry. Before I forget." I opened the top drawer of my desk and pulled out three necklaces.

"These are for protection. Do not take them off, even to bathe. I made them specially for you. When you shift they should shift with you."

Chuck and Cat each put one on. I bent down and put a tiny one on Fergus too.

"Hey, I get one too?"

"Of course you do, Fergus. You are part of us too. Think of it as bling." He ran to his barn to check it out in a mirror.

Chuck was trying to read the writing on the outside of the pendant. "What does it do?"

"It does three things. It works as a tracker so I can find you magically. There is a temporary shield in there that will last for thirty seconds. It needs a full hour to recharge. So if it activates get the hell out of there. It should stop most magical attacks. Notice I said 'most.' The last thing it does is monitor your health. If you are hurt, it will tell me. That is all it does, I swear."

"Agatha, I trust you." I looked over at Cat. She just smiled and nodded.

"OK, let's get this show on the road. Fergus, are you coming or staying with Chuck?"

The tiny Unicorn stuck his head out one of the barn's windows. "I get to choose this time?"

"You do. It could be dangerous but I'm going to Washington, DC. There have been some kidnappings and they need my magic to look into it."

He seemed to consider it for a moment. "If you're taking the Cat I better come along too. You need someone to watch her for you. Damn sneaky cats!" I had to smile as I picked him up. He slid into his pocket and was quickly peeking out the top.

Chuck reached down and gave Cat a peck on the cheek for which he received a punch to the shoulder. Cat's face was inflamed, and I kidded her about it all the way to the admin building. We looked a bit like backpackers on their way to a major hike. I had my clothing in my bag and carried a large duffel. Cat wore her pack and carried three more large bags. My supplies took up two.

"Ladies, are you ready to go?" I turned toward the voice just as I opened the front door to the building. Director Mills stood at the foot of the stairs behind us.

"We are. Do we have transportation?"

She smiled. "Follow me." She headed down the sidewalk that looped around the main building. The practice fields and obstacle course was along the way. I ran this route twice a week to keep in shape, but I wasn't loaded down with bags when I did that. Cat was barely breathing hard, and she carried three times the weight. Damn super-strong Weres.

As we cleared the edge of the building, I saw it. There was a UH-60 Blackhawk sitting in the middle of the soccer field.

"They must really want you, Aggy!" I looked back at my smiling friend. Neither one of us had ever been on a helicopter before.

"Nice ride Director."

"Isn't it? With all the road construction and a really big accident on the interstate they sent a helicopter. They weren't sure what you would be bringing, so they sent a larger one. Did you get everything you might need?"

"I did. I'm sure there are supplies available but they aren't mine. I'm sure this is a test of my abilities so whatever happens needs to be perfect."

The Director only nodded. She stopped while we were still out of range of the chopper and pulled me aside. "Agatha, be very careful of who you trust. Washington is a snake pit. I'm saying you could be in danger, but you and I both know what happened last week. You can trust Nita with your life. She is the best agent I know. Trust her. Now let's get you on board before they wonder what I'm telling you."

I looked over at Cat and our eyes met. I knew she heard everything and would remember it. As we approached the Blackhawk two male agents stepped out of it.

"Gentlemen, here are your charges. Meet Agatha Blackmore and Catherine Moore. Ladies, these are Agents Smith and Dale. They will get you to Washington and hand you off to Agent Lowrey. Be careful out there ladies. This is the big time."

The two male agents approached us and offered to take the bags. I smiled but told them no. I needed to keep an eye on my things at all times. Cat did allow them to help her put them up on the helo but like me kept control of them.

We secured the bags with strap down ties in the center of the craft. Cat and I sat next to each other facing the Agents. They gave each of us headsets that allowed us to hear what they were saying. The pilots were on a separate channel. This was not a combat mission so this Black Hawk wasn't armed except for the agents' sidearms. As we were not Agents yet, we were not allowed to carry for this mission. I made a mental note to ask Nita about that.

For as large as this helicopter looked on the outside there really wasn't all that much extra room inside it. If you squeeze them in, eleven men not counting the pilot can ride in here. Agent Dale was very talkative about the historical uses of the helicopter. He told us that this particular bird was used by the FBI almost exclusively. Its official designation was EH-60A instead of the UH-60. The difference was it was configured to handle both surveillance and tracking. The mounts for the computer stations were actually under our feet. He claimed that the engines had been upgraded and were actually faster than the standard model. He was about to go on when Agent Smith grabbed his arm and shook his head.

Both Cat and I were taking it all in. Any new knowledge was worth learning. We craned our heads to watch the ground go by as we flew. The noise created by the rotors was incredible, the headphones made a huge difference.

"So you're a witch? What makes you so special? We have worked with several magic users over the years and they are all the same." Agent Smith nudged his partner.

"Those are all Mercenaries. I'm in training to be an agent; they are just contractors."

"Sounds to me like you're just a couple of rich bitches looking for a ride to DC. How about you show us what you did to deserve the first class treatment? Come on. Show us!"

I switched to the pilot frequency. "Agents is this how you treat every guest on board a government aircraft?"

"Uh, Ma'am? You are on the wrong frequency. Channel two is what you are looking for." The co-pilot turned in his seat and tapped his helmet. "Ma'am, channel two is what you need." He raised two fingers and looked at me again. I nodded and smiled at him. I turned back to the Agents and smiled.

They glanced at each other, frowned and relaxed. I switched frequencies back to two. Children.

We had no further incidences for the rest of the flight. Washington looked pretty cool from the air. I remembered my reading and the lessons that Grams taught me about the founding of America. Many paranormals fled here with the early settlers. Europe was too crowded for our kind and the thought of a new world excited many of us. Many of those in the early magical communities influenced the mundanes in laying the foundations of liberty. It was easy to hide amidst the members of the Masons and Rosicrucians.

We landed at the heliport on the South parking entrance to the Pentagon. Since we were not going inside we didn't need an escort. There was a small building adjacent to the pad where we were to be met. Cat and I grabbed out bags without any help from the two 'Agents'. Hefting my duffel I led the way off the pad and down the sidewalk.

"Aggy, what was that with the frequency change?"

"I know for a fact that the pilot's frequency is recorded and monitored. Ours may not have been, and those two knew it. If something had happened, it would have been our word against two tenured agents. Now there is some inquiry on permanent record."

Cat nodded her head. "Smart."

The building contained only one person, and she was dressed like an Agent.

"Agent Lowery?" I held out my hand in greeting.

"Miss Blackmore. I have been waiting for you." The Agent clasped my hand gently. "And who is this?" She motioned toward a heavily laden Cat.

"Catherine Moore, my roommate and friend. She volunteered to help me with my supplies and serve as a bodyguard. She is the Alpha for her pack."

"Such a big title for a little girl. What clan and species are you?"

"WereCat. I don't have a registered Clan name yet, I just claimed the title recently."

"Interesting. Madeleine told me I could trust you."

"She said the same thing about you to us."

"At least we are on the same page. Would you like to go to your hotel and change? I know that helo was most likely not comfortable at all."

"Agent... Nita, we would rather go to the first crime scene. We didn't come here to take a vacation."

"That works for me. Let's get your stuff packed in my car. I have been meaning to ask why you two? What makes you so special? I've worked with magical people before."

I started to answer and Fergus did it for me. "Oh my god the noise is finally gone! Hey can't a man get a lift here?" I reached into my pocket and picked him up. Agent Nita's eyes about bugged out of her face at the sight of him.

"Whoa! Aren't you a big one? My name is Fergus. What is yours, pretty lady?"

"What is that?!"

Chapter 11

Nita was staring at Fergus like he was a demon from hell.

"This is Fergus. He's sort of my familiar and my friend. Fergus, say hello to Agent Lowrey."

"Hi there pretty lady, do ya like Unicorns?"

The agent peered at Fergus from all angles and then looked at me strangely. "So that is a real Unicorn? I thought they were like, bigger?" She held out her hands.

"He used to be."

"OK." She looked back at us and laughed. "I guess the Unicorn is what makes you special?"

"No, he's just along for the ride. I'm special because I'm a Witch and an FBI trainee. The Director said they asked for me?"

"Yes, they did. You said something to those two Senators that put this whole investigation on its ear. Can you tell me what that was?"

I sighed. So nice to have communications all on the same page. I explained what happened back at the school while we loaded the bags into her Suburban. It, like most government vehicles, was a darker shade of black.

"Now wait a moment. I've worked with dozens of Russian wizards or witches. I don't understand: they worked out just fine for me."

I climbed into the back seat, Cat wanted shotgun. "Who gave them their instructions? Was it you?" I struggled with the seat belt. It was a five-point harness, the first one

133

I had ever used. Cat had to lean over her seat to hook me up.

"It was my supervisor that gave them the orders. Hmmm. I don't remember ever giving them instructions ahead of time. They just show up, do the job, and then leave."

I nodded. "Someone in your field office knows the truth about them. That's interesting. It was a complete surprise to Madeleine." I looked around as we drove through the city. "Where are we going?"

"We know that there have been at least four kidnappings. These are politicos and diplomats. They hate both the press and the police. I'm taking you to the first crime scene out in Mount Vernon. Or at least what we think is the first. Senator Seymour Emery comes from old money. Really old money. There has been an Emery in the Senate for over a hundred years. His granddaughter was taken from inside his mansion while everyone slept. He has been the problem child in our investigation so far. He didn't involve us, his daughter did. He set his own investigators loose and has been riding the SAC of the investigation like a horse."

"Did we find anything at the mansion?" We had left the city behind us and were now headed down a country highway. In some ways the farms and fields reminded me of home.

"Our forensics team found nothing. The Magical team claimed they found traces of an intrusion, but the Senator's own people had muddled it too much, or so they claimed. We're stuck. The evidence, or rather the lack of evidence, has us stymied. What can you do that is different?"

I swear I'm going to make this my next lecture series. I could only shake my head. "What do you know about why the FBI uses Magical Mercenaries?"

Nita glanced back at me in the rear-view mirror. "I thought it was because the Witches' Council recommended them, but I'm not so sure now."

"You're wrong about that." I then gave her a short answer to her question. She glanced at both of us numerous times during the conversation.

"I hear what you're saying, I really do. But I don't believe you. I can't. It invalidates everything I have come to believe about the FBI and what I have witnessed during my own investigations. But I will keep an open mind for the next few days. The victims are what matters, not my opinions."

I nodded my agreement. Everyone was allowed to have an opinion. It was a mostly free country after all.

"Get ready: we are almost there. If you look to your right, you can see the roof of the house peeking over the ridge." Cat and I peered out the tinted windows at a half-dozen chimneys sticking up over the grassy hillside.

The road curved around a large hill and what I could only call a mansion came into view. Large iron-wrought gates gave way to a cobblestone paved courtyard in front of a large southern style house. Even though we were still in Virginia, the house looked out of place here.

"OK ladies. Into the lion's den we go."

I stepped out of the government vehicle and shivered. The temperature was at least fifteen degrees cooler than it was in the car. "Nita, do you need anything out of the car? I'm going to ward it. I have a few things in my bags I really need."

"It's a government vehicle; whatever is in there should be safe." I shrugged and motioned toward the car. "Fine." She reached inside and pulled out a small purse-like bag.

I pulled out a small piece of chalk and made a few marks on the stones and the tire of the car. Meditating for a moment I tossed a pinch of salt and herbs at the car and called upon Athena and Themis to protect the car from harm. Saying the word "gæta" I triggered my spell. Now if someone tried to tamper with the car, they would be stuck to it.

"Ready?" Nita was standing by the steps.

"Sure. Let's go." We climbed the short flight of stairs to the wrap-around porch. Large Corinthian columns framed the front door. All I could think of was 'stately Wayne Manor' as Nita rang the bell. I watched way too many reruns on TV with Fergus growing up.

The large front doors opened with a creak. Instead of Alfred we were confronted by a large - very large - man in a suit. "Yes?"

"Agent Lowrey and associates to see the Senator. Please." The man frowned but invited us inside.

"Stay here. I will inform him." The large man left us in a richly appointed foyer area. I took a moment to look around both with my eyes and my other senses.

"Agatha what do you see?" I opened my eyes and smiled at Cat.

"This house has wards; not real strong ones but they are here."

"What else?" I could tell she was encouraging me to think.

"There are spell traces from at least four different users. The door over there has a similar ward to what I use. It won't allow anyone in who wishes to harm the owner."

A loud booming voice suddenly said. "What did you say?"

I looked up and an elderly man was making his way down the stairs. "I said the ward on the front door will bar anyone who wants to harm the owner of the house. It is a very specific ward. I can sense one on the house that prevents fire and random destruction. Do you have similar ward on other doors and windows?"

"Why would I need those?" The man was shorter than Nita but less muscular than I was. His age was starting to show on his body.

"This Ward is very specific, and it only covers this room. Anyone could enter another way and not be bound by this one's rules."

"Agent Lowrey who is this young woman and why are you back in my house?"

"Senator Emery this is Agatha Blackmore, she is consulting on this case. Washington requested that she be allowed to examine the sites of the abductions. She is just going to attempt to trace the magic and then we are gone. I promise."

He nodded. "Fine. Just make it quick." The elderly Senator turned toward me and glared. "Young lady I will have you know that I paid good money for that Ward you are making light of. It is supposed to cover the entire house. If you are lying, I will make sure you never work in this country again! Damn mercenaries." He stormed up the stairs followed by the large guardian.

"Did he mean me or them?"

Agent Lowrey just rolled her eyes. She pointed to a door, and we opened it.

The door opened to a very nice living room or parlor. The layout was similar to my grandmother's house. Nita led us through to a hallway.

"The Senator's granddaughter used this section of the house as a playroom and guest room. The old man didn't like the noise or constant interruptions so he moved her down here. She was last seen in her bedroom. Most of her time was spent in the playroom." She pointed at the doors to the right.

"OK. Don't open either of them yet." I reached into the pouch at my hip and pulled out a small handful of herbs. In my head I ran through the steps for a diagnostic spell and said the words slowly. Both doors lit up with a faint glow. I carefully sprinkled herbs in the hallway.

"Both doors have a specific protection ward on them. This one is to protect the occupant no matter who it is. A good one for a child. Whoever laid it knew what they were doing." The door I pointed at was the bedroom door. It glowed with a faint green tint. "This other door is a problem. It has a ward but not one that protects a person. It is, so the room is not physically damaged. It's a vandalism spell." I reached out and opened the door to the bedroom.

Inside was obviously a child's room. Toys and kid's posters decorated the walls and antique furniture. There was a door on either side of the room. I held up my hands for everyone to freeze and I ran the diagnostic again.

Like before the inside of the door lit up as did all of the furniture. The window and doors remained unlit. "That is a problem. No wards on the window or those doors. The furniture is more of the vandalism spell." I opened the door on the right and it was a walk-in closet.

"We examined in there very carefully looking for trap doors or another exit. It's an old house, so we tried to be thorough. The windows showed no trace evidence and are painted shut from both sides."

The door on the left concerned me. I opened it and looked inside. The playroom was filled with toys and games. A high-end entertainment system dominated one corner of the room. We stepped inside. I ran through the spell a third time. Only the vandalism spell. But I was detecting another more subtle spell coming from the toy box along with a trace of some sort of lure spell left in the air. That one was extremely hard to see. Too many people and spells had covered it with trace elements.

I walked over to the large toy box and kneeled down. Remembering my forensic classes I pulled on a pair of gloves. The lid of the box was covered with stuffed animals. I began to remove them. Cat appeared next to me, put on gloves of her own and began to help.

"I'm pretty sure we searched those for her." I glanced over my shoulder at Nita.

Carefully I opened the lid of the box. It was filled with even more toys. Carefully I sifted through them. I felt a magical spark under my left hand and concentrated on that side of the box. Halfway down is where I found it. It was a finely crafted statue of what looked a bit like a dragon from a kids movie I once saw. It was about Hercules. Not wanting to touch it even with my fingers gloved, I reached into my pocket for a silk handkerchief.

Carefully I picked up the 'dragon' and slipped it into an evidence bag Cat held open for me. I looked up at Nita. "This might be our culprit right here."

"What is it? Other than a dragon." She peered at the statue through the bag.

"I'm not sure what it represents, but there is a spell embedded in it that acts as a lure spell. I sensed a trace of another similar spell here in the room. Too many people and other magic users have muddled it. All I can sense is its magic not what it did. This thing though is very insidious. It leaves you open to suggestion and messes with your belief in right or wrong. This wasn't random. She was targeted." Cat and I quickly refilled the box after taking a few pictures.

"How did our people miss this?" She was staring at the statue.

"It depends what they were looking for. I suspect they only looked for intrusion or teleportation traces."

"Is that even possible?"

"My grandmother has always claimed that it is. She did tell me that only the most skilled can even hope to accomplish it. One of the reasons she never gave the spell to me. I might end up on the moon if I tried it."

We found the Senator and a woman I assumed was his daughter waiting for us in the parlor. "Did you find anything?"

"Yes, Sir. We did." I could tell that Nita didn't want to answer him but he was a Senator.

The Senator sat up straighter. "What did you find?"

"Both rooms are protected by spells but only the one on the bedroom protected the child. The playroom only has the same vandalism spell that is on the furniture on it. The inner doors are not protected nor is the window. In the toy box we found a toy dragon with a coercion spell on it. Do you know where it came from?"

The mother covered her mouth with her hand as she gasped. "Which toy?"

I carefully pulled the bagged item out and showed it to her. "Please don't touch the bag. The item is very strong and will mess with your sense of judgment and morals."

"I have never seen that before. Where did it come from?"

"That is what we intend to find out. Senator does it look familiar?" The man barely looked at the bag.

"A toy is a toy. How is it you found it? I paid for the best Magic available."

"The FBI has access to someone better. We need to inform the task force and continue the investigation. Thank you for your time, Senator. We will be in touch when we learn more."

"Young lady when your contract is up with them, you call me. I will triple whatever they are paying you." I ignored his comment and shook my head at Cat.

"Ladies?" Nita motioned toward the door and we stepped out into the bright light of the afternoon. The Suburban sat right where we'd left it but it now featured a few new hood ornaments. Three men were attached to the car. One by each door and the third the hood.

Cat pulled out her camera and took pictures of the men. She was careful to get their faces and each one in the act of trying to break in. "It's a new record, Aggy!"

"For cars. We caught more than that at my lab. Nita, do you want me to release them or do you want to wait for local law enforcement?" She had a shocked look on her face.

She told me to wait and called a higher up for a decision.

"We can't take you anywhere, can we?"

"What about you? For a minute there I thought you were going to claw his face off."

"Nobody tries to buy my friends!" I had to chuckle: that wasn't exactly what he was doing, but I didn't correct her.

Nita got off the phone and looked at us. "My boss says let them go. Keep those pictures he wants to see them. It's political. Anyone else, I would have busted their ass for trying this!"

"Makes you wonder if they did it the first time you were here, doesn't it?" She gave me a sharp look.

"Next time I don't think I will do Madeleine any more favors. You two are trouble!"

Cat looked at her and laughed. "Me? I barely said two words in there."

"To me you two are a group. I've known you for only a few hours and I see this investigation is going to suck!"

I gave the men a last look and spoke "Frjáls." The men all dropped free of the car and fell to the ground. Nita stood looking down at the one by the driver's door as he woke up from the spell.

"Anywhere else you would be on your way to jail for this. Take this as your one and only warning." She stepped over him and climbed into the car. Cat and I followed.

We drove off leaving the men lying on the ground. "Where to next?"

"Well, the other Senators and the Mayor all live in a gated condo complex in Alexandria. We need to drop that thing off to the forensics team first. I don't want a repeat of that attempted break-in to damage the investigation. It worries me that they may have done that last time." She looked really annoyed.

The condo complex was back the way we came just inside the city of Alexandria. It was a large complex with high walls and security cameras everywhere. Somehow our kidnapper had gotten in and stolen the three children from right under the complex security's nose.

Nita showed her government identification to the gate guards, and they allowed us in. Three security breaches had them on a very high alert. The Senator from Georgia's home was our first stop as it was closest.

Security had called ahead and his personal guards were standing by at the door. They were not the same ones I had confronted at Quantico. Cat and I let Nita do all the talking, but we took note of how she did it. We were still students. The Senator was not in residence but his wife was. She greeted us immediately as we stepped inside.

"Agent Lowrey, do you think she's still alive?"

"Mrs. Payne, you know I can't comment on an open investigation, but we have nothing that says she is dead. We would like to take another look at her room and the house. Will you allow us to do that?"

"Of course! Anything that will help. Do you remember the way? I can have one of the guards show you."

"No thank you Mrs. Payne. I know the way. Thank you again." Nita made a 'come on' motion with her head and we followed her into the rest of the condo.

"She seems like a nice lady." Unlike the previous house this child's room was upstairs.

"She is. I just wish this was under better circumstances. The Senator and his wife have a room on the lower level. This whole floor is devoted to both their daughter and grandchild. Their daughter has cancer and has been in and out of hospitals for years. She has a bedroom up here too but rarely is here to use it." The top of the steps had a gate to prevent a child from falling down the stairs; it was open. The short hallway had three rooms and what looked like a bathroom. The door was open and I could see a sink.

Like last time I cast my diagnostic spell and sprinkled my herbs. All the doors lit up along with the walls and floor. "Wow! They went whole hog up here!"

I glanced at Cat and nodded. Concentrating, I could tell that the walls and floor spells were of a protection nature. They strengthened the structure of the house and prevented water breaks or earthquake damage. None of those would prevent a kidnapping. The door to the right was glowing orange. I carefully opened the door and looked inside.

144

"That is the mother's room. According to my notes she has not been here in some time." I nodded.

"Yes, the spells on the room are of a healing and regenerative type." I turned and looked at Nita. "There is no magical cure for cancer. All of this is a waste of money."

I opened the door on the other side. This room was warded, but not against kidnapping only for damage. I carefully scanned the room looking for magical traces. Like the other house there was something, but I couldn't get a line on what it was. The room itself was clean. "What is in the other room?"

"It's an entertainment area. They have game systems and a TV set up in there."

"I'm getting the same weird traces in the air that I got at the other house, but no sign of a lure. If it's here, that's where we will find it."

The recreation room was very nice. The games and toys were all carefully lined up and put away with care. The video setup was state-of-the-art. "This is a child's playroom?"

"She special. Marcie Payne has a form of Asperger's syndrome. She is very obsessive about her toys and other possessions. Everything has its place. At first we couldn't believe it was a kidnapping. Everything was too neat."

I remembered my reading. Asperger's meant she was higher functioning. I dropped into my meditative state and re-scanned the room. There was a slight trace of something on the display case in front of me.

"What's wrong with this picture?"

Nita came over to stand next to me. "There's something missing right there."

"Yes, there is. That was where our lure was located."

"Agatha? Can you come here a moment?" I stepped out of the room and went to Cat. She was just inside the bathroom door.

"What's up?"

Cat pointed into the bathroom and toward the bathtub. There, sitting on the edge of the tub was our missing statue.

"Nita? Cat found it."

"Is the same as the other one?"

"It feels the same." I placed it in an evidence bag. "Was Marcie bathing when she disappeared?"

Nita had her tablet out and was scanning through it. "I don't know. There was nothing said. We may have to re-interview the family. We did get lucky: Marcie labeled all of her possessions by date, time, and who gave it to her. The card on the shelf says that the dragon was a gift from 'Peter' at her sixth birthday party. Who is Peter? I need to call this in."

I scanned the bathroom just to make sure. The walls were reinforced like the rest of the rooms. The only part of the upper level that wasn't warded was the ceiling. No spells showed at all. I was staring at the ceiling when Nita returned.

"Nita? What's up there?" I pointed at the door in the ceiling.

"My notes say it's the attic. No fingerprints were found on the pull and nothing looked disturbed according to the agent who looked up there."

"It's the only thing up here not protected in any way. If Marcie was snatched out of her bath, the only way out with a wet and naked child would have been up. I can't be the only one who thought of that?"

"You're not. That was my idea, but the Russians said that it was impossible and found no trace on the door."

I sighed heavily. "When this is all over, Nita, I really need to finish my lecture on what Witches can and cannot do. Watch this please." I looked up at the door and telekinetically opened the door allowing the stairs to come down. I then grabbed Cat with my mind and she began floating up toward the hole. I carefully set her down and looked at Nita. She had her mouth open.

"That was telekinesis and about all I can do for the rest of the day. I only have a minor talent in that. This is how she was taken. Somehow they got her out of the attic. We just have to look. Dust can also be moved by someone with enough skill. You weren't there but this jives with what the Russians said back in Director Mill's office. They took her through the roof."

"Damn. OK. I will call it in, again. I'm going to request a full team out here again. Let's wrap this up and get over to the other condos. This proves we have a serial kidnapper or something like it."

CHAPTER 12

We found statues in all the children's homes. The forensics lab said that no trace evidence other than the children's was found on any of them. Initial investigators missed them because they looked like toys. The lead agent on the case was blaming the Russian Mercenaries for the misstep. They still didn't understand how those guys operated. I tried to keep my opinion to myself about it all. My FBI career hadn't even started yet and here I was about to make waves.

They set up a command center in the parking lot of the complex. The forensics van and techs couldn't be hidden this time. The news media swarmed like bees to honey outside the walls. Cat and I sat watching the circus from outside the command center. So far they had excluded us. I suspected that we would be included, eventually. At least they had food. I knew Fergus was hungry.

"It's about damn time you remember to feed the Unicorn! I could have starved to death in your pocket. Look I'm already wasting away!" He was turning his head and trying to see his backside.

"You can afford to lose a little weight. You've had too many pizza parties with Chuck."

The mini Unicorn put his nose in the air and snooted. "I have no idea what you're talking about."

"So you deny ordering Pizza and salad from that place in town. What is it called? Anchors a Weigh? Shall I call your little girlfriends Jody and Anne and tell them no more orders?"

"How did you know about Anchors a Weigh?" He was peering up at me.

"The empty pizza and salad boxes were a bit of a giveaway but it was Grams who ratted you out. Pretty sneaky charging it to your phone bill. She said to tell you the chef salad three times a week is not a long distance call. She said if you want to keep doing that you have to call her and ask permission each and every time from now on."

"Sorry, but I was hungry." He hung his head and then looked up at me with puppy-dog eyes.

"Not falling for it this time, mister."

"Wait, is that how Chuck has been getting all the pizza? I've smelled it on him and couldn't figure out where it was coming from." Now Cat was staring at him too.

"Fergus, I bring you plenty of hay and other things that Unicorns are supposed to eat. Not Chef's salads and pizza!"

"Hey, bro's before ho's!"

"Eat your salad. We will talk about this later when we get home." He turned away from us and pretended he didn't hear me anymore. Unicorns.

"Hey Aggy?"

I looked away from Fergus. Cat was staring at our Suburban, several people were peering in the windows.

"Did you secure the car like last time?"

"I did. This should be fun to watch."

Cat nodded.

The first applicant tried the door handles to see if they were locked. He tried all four doors and the rear hatch. He even checked the skylight to see if it was open. With his companions acting as lookouts he pulled out a lock-pick and tried to pick the lock. I laughed when after a moment one of his companions had to shake him.

"Are you going to let them get away?"

"Let who get away?"

We both looked up and said in unison. "Hi Nita."

"Who are you letting get away?"

Cat pointed at the car. "Those guys."

Before she could yell, I waved my hand and said. "Frjósa" The two men froze in the act of running away.

Nita looked down at us as we ate our food and laughed. "You two are a laugh riot."

"We were hungry."

"Is it just the three of them?"

"So far. Want to wait for more guys?"

"No, let me call it in. Can't take you anywhere…"

I looked over at Cat. "Still want to be an FBI agent?"

"I still do. We can do better than these guys. I can't believe that they are this ignorant about para's after a hundred years of exposure to us."

"I know… Oh, look there's Nita." Nita was now standing in front of our Suburban staring at the three frozen men. Standing next to her were three new Agents.

"Can you hear what they are saying?" Cat was the freaky hear-it-all.

"Yeah. That older Agent is yelling at Nita. It seems he is the one that sent them after her car."

"He is? Why did they try to break in, then?"

"That's what she just said. He's saying that he wants our things searched for evidence!"

"What! That's not going to happen. Over my dead body!"

"Nita is calling somebody. The other guy just called over a couple of mercs and told them to break into the car!" Cat turned toward me, her eyes wide. "Can they?"

"I'd like to see them try." I reached into my pocket and pulled out a small bag. Ever since I took it from the strong box in my lab I had thought about it. According to Grandmother, her Grandmother had been an enforcer for the council back in the old world of Europe. A family heirloom had been passed from mother to mother in the hopes that one would take it up. It was only for those who sought justice in the world. Grams had given it to me for when I made my final decision and graduated as an FBI agent at long last. I still wanted that goal and like Cat, thought I could make a difference. Inside the bag was a bracelet. It was more of a cuff, but once it was on, I would not or could not remove it. It, like the job, was a personal trust, something I could not take lightly. Watching agents who should be working together to find stolen children fight over pettiness and blame irritated me to no end. It made me want to exact justice.

"That's pretty."

I looked down at the shiny bracelet. "Thanks. Grams gave it to me. She said it would make me a better person. It belonged to her grandmother. She was an enforcer for the European Council. I haven't felt myself to be worthy of it until now. Watching them has made me want the job even more." I slipped it onto my right wrist and locked the clasp. It constricted all on its own and the locking mechanism vanished. It was now one continuous band.

"Cool. What does it do?"

"Not a clue!"

"Only you, Agatha... Only you would put a magical artifact on your arm that someone gave you not knowing what it does." I just smiled at her. My wrist tingled, but that was all the bracelet seemed to do so far.

Nita finished her phone call and looked at the older agent who smirked at her. She crossed the parking lot and stopped at our table.

"I assume you heard some of that. My superior said that he is within his rights to search the car."

"Nita, are Cat and I subject to his orders?" The mercenary magicians were circling the car looking for a weak spot.

She thought for a moment. "You aren't. The Academy sent you to the investigation on orders from my boss. You only answer to him and through him, me. Agent Mu over there can't control you."

I laughed. "His name is Moo? Like a cow?"

"Cows? Keep those big ugly things away from me. All they do is eat and poop. It's never ending. Did I tell you about the farm I was on before I got turned into a toy? They had cows and pigs; talk about stink!"

"Fergus, be quiet." I picked him up and stuck him in my pocket.

"No, his name is Leeroy Mu spelled with a 'u'. He is a Senior Agent so I technically have to do as he says unless I have other orders from higher."

"I like Moo better." I sat up in my chair and peered across the lot. The Russians must have found the surprise I left in the shield. Grandmother always said it was easier to catch a rat with cheese than with vinegar.

"Nita take a seat this should be fun to watch."

The Russians cast a removal spell that took three of them to cast. They yelled something to Agent Mu. Mu looked at one of the agents milling around and told him to open the car up. He reached for the door and was promptly stuck. Frozen as if in amber. I burst out laughing.

The mercenaries could hear me and glared at me. I was polite and only smiled back.

"How many agents do you think they will waste trying to get into my spell supplies?"

"Is that what is in those bags? They can buy that stuff anywhere. Why try so hard?"

"You can't buy my stuff. Some of the items in those bags are worth more than this command center." I thumped the big bus we were leaning up against.

"You might want to tell Mooby that he's too close to their casting. Oops too late." A stray bolt of lightning just missed making Moo a Mooette.

The agent in question crossed the lot and approached our table. "Agent Lowery, I demand that you order them to lower that ward so we can inspect their bags for stolen items!"

Cat reached under the table and laid a hand on my leg. I had been about to say something. This was a dominance battle. If there's one thing a Were would know about its dominance.

"What stolen items would those be? Who is making the accusation?"

"I don't have to tell you that! Do as I say: that's an order."

The three Russians came up behind Moo and started talking to me. "Glupaya ved'ma"

"Poluchit' etot shchit vniz yeshche?" All three of them glared at me.

"What is she saying to them?" Moo looked a bit put out.

"Not a clue. I don't speak Russian."

"Yesli Sovet Ved'my uznayet, chto vy kradete oni naydut vas i polozhit' konets vas." I drew a finger across my throat. All three of them got very anxious and looked to Agent Moo to save them.

"What are you saying to them? I demand you tell me!"

"All I said was if the Witches' Council knew they were stealing things, that they would be in serious trouble. More or less."

"What have they stolen?"

"My stuff in the car. It's mine. Not theirs."

"Whatever is in the car is the property of the US Government! Now drop that shield now!"

"What in the hell is going on out here?" All the agents turned to their right and grimaced. Three United States

Senators and the Mayor of Alexandria were standing in the parking lot staring at Agent Moo Moo.

"Senators, Mr. Mayor, we are just having a small difference of opinion and I will be with you in a moment."

"Excuse me? Agent Mu? We would like to know what is more important than our children's lives?!"

"We had a report that these young women stole something from one of the residences and we are trying to search that vehicle."

Senator Payne stared at Moo like he was crazy. "And that is more important than my daughter? Isn't this the young lady that found the thing that ties this all together? The thing that your investigation missed?"

"Senator I can't comment on an active investigation..." He didn't have time to finish his statement before his phone rang. He looked at the display and excused himself.

Cat smiled at me and tapped her ear.

Agent Mu looked a bit pale when he stepped back to the Senators. He handed his phone to Agent Lowery and stepped back.

"Hello? Yes, Sir. No, Sir. He's an asshole sir. Yes, sir. Yes, Sir. I do believe they heard me Sir. Yes, Sir. Thank you, Sir. Right away." She handed Mu his phone back. "Do I have to say it?"

"No." Mu turned and left the area.

"That was Director Turton. I'm now in charge. Back to work all of you. Ladies?"

Nita turned to the Senators. "Sorry about all of that. We will find them. I have our best people on it." She shook all of their hands and stepped back to us.

"What do you want us to do?"

"Agatha, can you get with the forensics team and see if you can figure out what we are dealing with? Cat can go with you to watch your back. I need to go fire some Russians."

<<<>>>

The portable forensics lab was inside a large moving truck parked behind the command center. Cat followed me as we weaved around the vehicles to find the entrance to it.

"Chuck is going to be big time jealous that he missed this! This is his thing."

"Well maybe next time he can guard me instead of you."

Cat looked, and me and laughed. "Nah."

"Yeah, didn't think so." I found the door and knocked. A white-coated lab tech opened the door.

"We've been sent to help."

"We don't need help." "SAC Lowery said to help you. Have you figured out what spell is on it yet?"

The tech opened the door, and we stepped inside. The four statues were lined up on a glass table. Techs in lab coats were examining them looking for external clues. A team of two Russian mercenaries were standing against the wall peering at the one at the end.

"Figurnyye yego yeshche?" The Russians looked at me and shook their heads.

"Nyet."

"Eto primanka. Eto zastavlyayet vas brosit' svoyu okhranu i stolovykh s chuvstvom suzhdeniya." The two

157

stopped and started to nod their heads. Then they shrugged.

"Voznikayet vopros: pochemu?"

"Uh, what is she saying to them?" One of the techs came over to Cat.

"What I told them is the statues are a form of lure. They somehow disturb humans and mess with your judgment. Your sense of right or wrong. It's a very intricate spell, but it doesn't make any sense. Why use it?"

"Who are you?"

"Agatha Blackmore. I located those for you. I really wouldn't be touching them with your hands. Just a suggestion." The lab techs in question froze and carefully set them down.

I stepped closer to the table and peered at one of the dragon figures. I felt a shiver up my right arm and saw my new bracelet flash red for just a second. Interesting.

"Have you figured out what they represent?" The lab guys all stopped and stared.

"She means the actual figures not the magic. Are they from mythology or something?" Cat for the save.

"Yes, we traced the iconology to a fifteenth century text. It's not a hydra as we first thought but a dragon. The heads are all different; dog, griffin, and man."

"What text was it in? And what does it refer to?"

"It is an early Christian work by Johann Weyer, called De Praestigiis Daemonum et Incantationibus ac Venificiis."

Crap! "Gentlemen that is a very rare and very scary book about demons. What demon does it represent?"

"My Latin is a little sketchy but the name that leaps out at me is Bune." It didn't ring a bell but grandmother only touched on the major demons.

"Any other more modern references to be had?" I pulled out my cell phone and frantically texted Grams about a three-headed dragon representing a Demon named Bune.

"Just one by Mathers."

"Key of Solomon Mathers?"

"Yes. He says that Bune gives riches, wisdom, and eloquence. And that he can answer questions truthfully."

"Crap on a stick. We need Agent Lowery in here. Right now!" My cell phone rang, and I answered it.

"Aggy what are you mixed up in? Bune is a high powered Duke of Hell. His followers were called Bunis. You remember what I taught you about demons. Don't worry about the Council, I will update them."

The Russians came up to me and began asking questions. "What is happening? What you find out about spell?"

"Chto vy znayete o demonakh?" They couldn't get off the truck fast enough. They just about knocked Nita down as they ran for the hills.

"Agatha, is there a reason why two Russians just about knocked me down on my way in here?"

"We figured out what it is we are dealing with."

"Don't all tell me at once...! What is it?"

"Demons. Someone is trying to raise one again."

"Crap! We run into something like this about once or twice a year. Most never get so far as to have victims or potential victims. Do you know what Demon it is?"

"Bune. One of the Dukes of Hell. That statue is a dragon that represents him."

"One question; or rather one big question. How did these kids get these and why them?"

Chapter 13

"What do we know about the parents and grandparents? Is there something that they all share?" Both Nita and I turned and stared at Cat.

"What? It's basic police work. I do pay attention in class sometimes." I looked at Nita and spread my arms.

Nita turned and went back to the command center to check on that. She had been finding that Agent Mu had not really been doing his job. With no evidence, he had not believed it was a kidnapping and was off in left field looking for runaways.

I looked at the forensic techs. They all looked tired. "Let's all take a break? Half of you go eat something and relax for a bit. Come back in an hour, then we will switch." The tired techs nodded and left to go eat. With half the people gone the lab looked very empty. The forensics lab was pretty cool. It was based upon a semi-truck using technology associated with recreational vehicles. Both sides of the cargo area were slides that when deployed doubled the inside floor space. Every conceivable piece of equipment available that would fit was inside. Power was supplied by a large towed generator and a solar panel array on the roof. A radar dish similar to that used by news crews was also deployable from the roof. It was a very comprehensive vehicle.

"That was a good idea." One of the techs sitting behind a computer was looking at us.

"Everyone looks so tired. They needed a break. Cat and I have been sitting outside at a table since you guys got here. They wouldn't let us help. We are still students, remember?"

"That's right, I forgot about that. Technically, I'm the one in charge around here but I rarely pull rank. I just suggest things and they do it. Agent Mu gave us explicit orders to work this case, so we got lost in it. We haven't been introduced, have we? Agent Anastasia Moondragon." She held out her hand to me and I took it. Her hand was very cool to the touch. I glanced at her face and looked closer. It could have been the light but her skin was very pale and washed out looking.

I smiled at her and took a chance. "Vampire?"

"Very good Miss Blackmore. Not many get it on the first try. Yes I am a Vampire. One of very few in the FBI these days. You might say the Forensic Department is my domain since I rarely leave the truck."

"I'm so sorry I just charged in and started giving you orders! I just want to find the kids."

Anastasia started to laugh. "I want to find them too. That's why I let you. Besides, you breathed a bit of fresh air into the room. We get stuffy and focus on the wrong things sometimes." She turned her attention toward Cat. "I can tell what you are but not the species."

"WereCat. Catherine Moore, nice to meet you." Cat held out her hand.

"I would say you are an Alpha too. Not all that many female Alphas running wild out in the world. Welcome to the FBI." Cat could only stare.

"Don't look so shocked. I've been around for a while. Never worked with a Witch before, or at least not a sanctioned Witch. The Russians don't count. They don't care for me or I them. Too much history there."

"Anastasia, were you alive during the Demon War?"

"Well, not alive. But yes, I was around then. I joined the FBI during the summer of love in 1969 on a whim. This is not the first time since then that we have come across demon influences, but it appears to be the most organized. I've got the system searching for a manufacturer or supplier for those things. They look like they may be mass produced. If so, we can trace the shipments."

"Have you tried local artists? Maybe it was done locally."

"That's a good idea... I will add it to the search." She typed on her computer for a bit then looked up at us. "Anything else?"

"I don't think so. Do you mind if we go check out what Agent Lawson is working on?"

"Ladies you don't have to ask me, you aren't one of my charges. Good work by the way. I'll let you know if we find anything."

I grabbed Cat by the arm and we exited the lab. "Did you know she was a vampire?" I couldn't believe I had just met one!

"She smelled like damp earth and Cinnamon. I've never smelled a combination like that on a human before so I knew she was something else. But I've never met a vampire before either. Chuck is going to be big-time jealous! Imagine an FBI tech on the job for over forty years? She must have an incredible amount of knowledge."

The command vehicle was directly behind the massive forensics lab. The truck was more than half the size. I knocked on the door and waited for someone to answer.

"Yes?" The Agent that answered the door was a large man with grey hair and deep-set eyes. What surprised both Cat, and I was that he was wearing shorts.

He saw us laugh, and he smiled. "It gets hot in here. What can I do for you ladies?"

"Is Agent Lowery inside?"

He checked our badges to make sure we were who we said we were and let us in. The area inside was tight with computer stations lining the walls. The center of the room was set up with a video conferencing station and a map plot complete with whiteboards and research areas. Despite three air conditioning units the place was very warm.

Nita was hunched over a computer station with another Agent reviewing information on the screen. "Nita?"

"Hello ladies, how was forensics? Anastasia didn't give you too hard of a time did she?"

"No, Ma'am she didn't. We came to see if you found anything about a Bune cult or whatever."

"Well, no cults as far as we can tell. It's not illegal to worship demons so we don't track religious groups. Only those that have caused problems or have been arrested before. Records show that Bune worshipers have popped up on our radar once before. In the early 1990's the FBI stopped a rogue Bune group from influencing a presidential campaign. Once we shut them down the candidate stopped making sense to the public and was defeated fairly easily. The gift of eloquence is real. We have been searching the backgrounds of our Senators and the Mayor looking for some sort of commonality that links the four. So far we have nothing. All government officials are scanned very carefully for demonic influences these days. We learned our lessons from both the 1960s and the 1990s incursions. Demons cannot be allowed to influence politics or government."

"So nothing links them at all?"

"They all belong to some of the same charity groups and two of them are in the same Masonic lodge. Masons are different. They follow a specific creed and are bound in fellowship. We have investigated lodges before and found them to be benign."

I nodded. "Grandmother once told me that Masons were building the temple in the next life. We should be ashamed for suspecting them. But everyone is suspect when the life of a child is involved, much less four. What about the wives?"

"We checked them too. No links that we could find. They all went to different colleges. Each came from a different part of the country. Most were married right out of college and are the perfect politician's wives."

"Stepfords?" Nita gave Cat a sharp look.

"Fictional movies and books aside there has only been one case of real so-called Stepfords and that was in France of all places. The reports that we have are they used flamethrowers against them and the entire cult was destroyed before they could do any more damage. No, this is something else entirely. But good guess!"

I stared at the screens and then glanced at the whiteboards. My new wristband twitched. I had an idea that the whatever-it-was bracelet agreed with.

"What about the mothers of the children? How do they match up with their parents? What do they have in common other than being family? I might be saying this wrong."

Nita made a face and began typing. "How the mothers and fathers relate to the parents? What they have in common? Is that what you mean?"

"I was studying the whiteboard information and something rang a bell. Because the children live with politicians, we have assumed the kidnappings were political. But what if they aren't? Have we checked out the mothers? Or maybe how the mothers relate to their parents?"

Nita looked around the room. "OK everybody I want two teams. Half of you start researching the grandmothers, the other half the mothers. I want links between the two up on the board, let's move people."

I stepped closer to the agent. "Nita, why take us so seriously? We aren't even agents yet."

"You found something that veteran agents missed more than once. None of us saw what was right in front of us. You both have fresh eyes and powers we don't understand. Maybe, just maybe, you have some insight we can use."

That made sense. I stepped over to the boards and began adding the information as it came in. Nothing matched up. The mothers went to different schools, grew up in different states, and even belonged to different charity organizations. Three of the mothers went to different colleges than their parents, but the one that did was the one with the medical condition. Whatever the link, it wasn't something obvious. It was very frustrating.

Then Nita got a call from forensics and we had our first break in the case.

"Anastasia traced the maker of those statues! It's a local manufacturing plant here in Alexandria. Want to come along?"

Warrants were acquired in a hurry. Possible Demonic activity was a guaranteed way to get them. Two tactical teams hit the plant just as they closed down their operations for the day. A team of agents served the warrants to the front of the building while tactical came in the rear and from the side. Many of those inside thought it was an immigration raid, and all exited as fast as possible. Fortunately the building itself was surrounded by a ten - foot chain-link fence with one gate in or out. Those that tried to climb to get away were easily apprehended.

Cat and I went in last along with Agent Lowrey to interrogate the owner and manager who happened to be the same person.

"... I had no idea that many of my workers were illegal! As far as I knew they were OK; I mean, they had proper documentation. I don't understand this, INS was just here last week."

"Mr. Dawn this has nothing to do with INS. We will be informing that agency about the results of this raid, but we have nothing to do with any of that. What we require is

167

any information about these." Nita laid four pictures in front of the man of the dragon statues.

He studied the statues for just a moment and looked up. "The hydras? Those were a special order for a new customer. I would need to check my records but we did those about a month ago. Short run, guy said they were for a fantasy group I think."

"Do you remember what he looked like or anything about the man?"

"Like I said I would need to check my records. I just remember the dragons. We make lots of stuff like that." Nita looked at the milling agents. "Someone take Herman here and pull the records for that order. Get everything."

Two of the larger agents took the man in tow and went to his office. Nita looked over at me. "Agatha would you do that diagnostic spell of yours and check the warehouse and offices? See if there is anything out of order around this place. Cat, tag along with her and check for unusual smells as well."

As we headed into the warehouse proper Cat mentioned that she didn't want us to be Team "Scratch and Sniff."

I sank into my meditation and cast the diagnostic spell again. This time small spikes of magic lit up around the small factory. With Cat in tow we poked and prodded the machinery and molding systems. I found small traces of magic and what might be called a whiff of a psychic trail that I followed back to the owner's office.

Nita and some of the forensic techs were there along with Mr. Dawn.

"So you don't remember anything about the man that ordered these?" Nita waved the pictures at the Herman again.

"Well, no. He was only here three times. The first to place the order and later to pick it up. He came by when we first started to press the molds. It was a quality control check is what he said."

"So three times and you can't describe him? Is that what you are saying, Herman?"

Herman shook his head and repeated his answer.

"What about the cameras? Did they get a picture of him?" I was looking at the hidden camera inside the picture on the wall.

"Cameras? What cameras?" Nita looked at Cat and I.

"Behind you, in the picture." One of the techs lifted the picture of an older woman off the wall. Embedded in the frame was a small multi-angle camera lens.

Nita looked at us and smiled. "Thank you Agents."

She called us Agents which made my day. The whole experience back at the Academy had made me hypersensitive when it comes to cameras. I looked for them everywhere.

"Where's the receiver and memory storage, Herman?"

The man sighed and pointed at the potted plant next to the door. "Look under the plant."

"Herman, Herman, Herman we were just looking for the statues, but now we need to see what else you have cooking around here. Naughty naughty."

That reminded me. "Agent Lowrey, we found spell traces in the warehouse but most of them are small equipment tweaks and repairs that are benign at best. I followed a magical trail that had a familiar psychic scent into this office."

"What is it?"

"I'm not sure. It started at the molding machines and runs back to this room. I need to run another spell."

"Do we need to clear the room?"

"I don't think so. I've gotten better at the spell." I slipped back into my trance and triggered the spell. I was starting to run out of salt, it's a good thing I'd brought almost fifty pounds of it with me.

"There are traces of whatever it is in the room but the strongest is coming from under his desk. I think there is a floor safe or a hidey hole of some kind under there."

The desk was moved and carpet ripped up. Set into the floor was a small metal door with a digital lock embedded into it.

"OK Herman. Give us the combination."

He shook his head and replied. "No more help."

The techs told Nita they could drill the lock but the best way would be to remove the whole safe. That would take anywhere from hours to days to get inside.

"Cat, can you give it a try?"

We all watched as my roommate, this little slip of a girl, walk over to the safe grab the handle and give it a jerk. The door of the safe came off in her hands with a loud clang. She handed it to one of the techs who had taken a huge step back from her.

"Thank you. Agent Moore." Cat gave Nita the cutest smile.

The forensic techs began to reach into the safe when I caught a whiff of what they were removing. "Freeze! Agent Lowrey, I have demonic traces just like the statues in there!"

The lab techs turned sheet white and backed slowly away from the hole in the floor. No one wanted to be locked away forever as being possessed.

I approached the hole and looked down. Carefully I telekinetically removed the items one at a time. A large bundle of money, jewelry, some odds-and-ends gemstones, and a small bag of what looked like coins. The coins were the danger.

"It's the coins. That other stuff has a faint glow about it but it's from contact with the coins. That glow should fade with time. Just store them separately and wear silk gloves if you have to touch them. The coins are another thing altogether. They are demonically enhanced."

Nita grabbed Herman and dragged him over to the desk. I levitated the small bag and set it in front of him. Without opening the bag I could see they looked like gold.

"What are they and where did you get them? Let me tell you up front a few things. Demon worship is not illegal, but kidnapping is and if you don't start talking right now, you are our only lead on four child abductions. You are looking at going away for a very long time."

Dawn was sheet white. "Demons, Kidnapping, what the hell are you talking about? The man came in here to order the statues, he wanted twenty of them. Special he said. He paid up front and gave us all the designs and mold settings. He showed up the day of casting out of the blue and said he wanted those coins embedded inside the statues. I was like 'Sure, anything you want.' We poured the mold, and he watched as the coins went into the first batch. He slapped me on the back and left. I checked out the coins, saw they were solid gold and thought payday! I kept the rest and put washers in place of them in the other statues. How was he going to know? Right? He came back, picked up the order, and left."

Nita could only shake her head at this guy. "Get him out of here. Agatha, can you get those to Anastasia? I don't feel safe letting the regular human techs touch them."

I nodded and reached into the backpack Cat was wearing. I had packed several silk bags to use for carrying artifacts or spell components. I carefully lowered the coins into the bag and then sealed them into an evidence bag. The forensics truck was just pulling in as we walked out of the building. Since the FBI had seized this warehouse and fenced area, it made a perfect spot to work from. Easy security once the cars were removed from the lot.

To preserve the chain of evidence, I handed the bag to Anastasia personally and watched as she signed for it. Procedure was very important in our job.

She got to work immediately analyzing the coins and looking for trace evidence. Other techs had the camera footage and were scanning for familiar faces and looking for our guy.

The techs found several underworld representatives and a drug runner on the tapes which explained why they were hidden. The DEA and RICO boys would find much of this very interesting, but it didn't get us closer to our kidnapper.

Finally the tape rolled past a man I thought I recognized. "Stop. That guy. Back up a bit."

The man in the picture was a very large man in a suit. The cameras were set too low the catch his face in the first scene. On the second visit they only caught his back and front of his shirt. The final shot was of him and Herman shaking hands. He leaned down to pick up the box of statues and his face was revealed.

"We've seen him before! It's Senator Emery's servant!"

Chapter 14

Senator Seymour Emery's house was the first crime scene we'd visited. The man on the screen was the one who both answered the door and escorted him back up the stairs. This was bad. Senator Emery was a major mover and shaker in DC. He had a lot of money and was not afraid to use it. His was also the house where men attempted to break into our vehicle. This had the potential to be a political nightmare.

The command center was tightly filled with all the agents involved. "What do we know?" Nita looked very tired.

I looked to the whiteboards and studied them. The other agents filled in Nita with what we knew and didn't know. Our prime suspect was a member of the Senator's own household. According to background checks run by Agent Mu's team his name was Aalu Kovacic. He was of Croatian descent and had worked for the family for many years. We knew that the Senator was conducting his own investigation and had attempted to break into an FBI vehicle. Agent Mu was now being investigated for both that and some of his other orders by the FBI's version of Internal Affairs. We had the statues and knew how they were constructed. But we had no proof connecting the Senator to the investigation. Only his hired help.

"Can we get a warrant to search the house?" Agent Smith, one of the original team members, voiced the question we were all thinking.

"With the evidence we have? I doubt it. He allowed us access to the child's rooms before, but if he finds out we suspect him, he will cut that off quickly. Pull everything we have into a readable report. I will send it higher. This is going to suck." She looked over at Cat and I. We were just about asleep leaning against the wall.

"Agent Smith, take temporary Agents Moore and Blackmore to the hotel and get them settled. Ladies, we will come for you when we have something actionable. So get some rest. You deserve it."

We thanked Nita and followed Agent Smith out to our Suburban. A quick snap of my fingers dropped the shield I'd put up. The agent glanced at our bags piled in the back and told us to hop in.

"What hotel are we going to?" I was in the back watching the cars go by.

"We have rooms reserved at the King's Inn for stay-over visitors. You two deserve it. For students you ask good questions."

"Thank you Agent Smith. I studied everything I could get my hands on about the FBI when I was given the choice to join. Cat there is the same way. A friend of ours, Chuck, reads even more than we do."

"It sounds to me like you have the makings of a good team. From what I remember from the Academy you may get that opportunity. Hold on to him or some other team may try to steal him."

Cat almost growled. "They can try."

The agent looked back at me in the mirror. I explained. "Cat is his Alpha. She is a bit possessive about some things."

Remembering the floor safe the agent could only nod. "There: your hotel." He pointed to a multi-story building on the left of the highway.

We didn't have to check-in and Cat was able to carry the bags in. We said goodbye to the agent and got settled in. Our rooms were connected by a door. The room was on the third floor but I set my standard wards, anyway. I had just finished when Cat came in through the door. "Hey, whatcha doing?"

"I'm setting the wards for the rooms. Let me know if you want to go outside and I will make a hole."

"Is it the same kind of ward you put on the car?"

"It's a bit similar. The ward I put on the auditorium is just like it. Anyone of ill intent cannot get inside. We are safe here."

"Thanks for bringing me along, Aggy. This has been fun."

"You're just happy you got to show off in front of all those agents."

She rolled her eyes at me.

"Why don't you call Chuck and rub it in? You know he has to be dying to know what we've done and who we've met. We can't talk about the case, but we can mention Anastasia the Vampire."

Cat ran back into her room and grabbed her cell phone. I could hear her chatting with Chuck and laughing. Fergus looked over at me from the table in the room. "Is hay all you brought? I could go for a salad right about now."

I gave him a 'really?' look.

"Just saying. I've been listening to you and those FBI guys all day. And I had an idea on how you can get into the house."

At this point any idea, even one that comes from a Unicorn, might be a good one. "What is your idea?"

"Use the daughter, the mother of Senator Memory's granddaughter. Isn't she the one that called the FBI originally, anyway?"

"It's Senator Emery and yes she is. I will mention that to Nita. Good idea Fergus." I laid out on the bed and flicked on the TV. Center stage in the news was the kidnappings. It only took a day for them to ferret out the reason for the investigation. So much for secrecy. There were camera shots of the FBI vehicles and some of the agents walking around. I didn't like what the one reporter said about how insiders report that 'Magical support brought in by Washington had sidelined the investigation'. That was a prod at Cat and I. Although completely untrue it could hurt Nita. I looked up her number and dialed.

She picked up after three rings. "Agatha is something wrong?"

"No we are OK. Did you see the news? What they are saying about Cat and I?"

"Calm down. We know it's not true. Washington knows that it isn't true. I checked with my boss. It seems that after Agent Mu was interviewed by internal review, he called a friend of his at the Post and spilled his guts about the investigation. He's right out of the FBI. They revoked his credentials two hours ago. Charges are pending and he won't be able to wriggle his way out of them at all."

"Oh, OK. I was worried. How goes the case?"

"Not good. My boss says we don't have enough to go against the Senator. He wields too much power in Congress to hit head on. Any hint of an investigation and he will come down very hard on us. We have to have solid evidence to even try."

"Fergus had an idea on how to get inside the house."

"Fergus, the Unicorn?"

"Occasionally a gem of truth falls out of his ass but yes the Unicorn has an idea."

"Do I really want to know?"

"It's not a bad one. What he suggested is that we use the child's mother. She is the one that called us in the first place. We could go to her with either our suspicions or use her to get to the bodyguard."

"That's actually not a bad idea. I will say it came from you though. I really don't want to write in my notes that a mouse-sized Unicorn is making the decisions here. Get some rest. I'll send an agent for you in the morning."

I relayed the information to Cat. She ended up in my room on the other bed. We both felt the big rooms were too much for us alone. The day had been incredibly long and both of us were very tired. I'm not sure what woke me up first, the man stuck to my window or my new bracelet.

I was so sure it was a dream. I heard a loud thump followed by my wrist getting suddenly warm and almost vibrating. For a moment I thought my cell phone was in bed with me. Then I heard the second thump. "Cat! Did you hear that? Cat?" I threw a pillow at my friend and roommate.

179

"Why is the rum gone? Wait... What? Did you throw a pillow at me?"

"Did you hear that?" I cocked my head to one side.

"You know I can hear everything. What is it I'm listening for?" There was yet another thump this time followed by a loud scraping noise and then a crash.

Cat looked at me and pointed toward the windows. "That noise? Yes. I heard something. Can I go back to sleep now? Maybe he's still on the island waiting for me." She fell back and covered her face with a pillow.

I looked at the clock. It read five in the morning. I blinked a few times to clear the sleepy out of my eyes. I crawled out of the nice warm and toasty sheets and pulled the drapes aside to look out. I screamed and jumped backwards!

"What! What is it!" Cat sat up in bed and was in a half-change. Her face contorted and changed as large needle teeth appeared and her eyes began to change.

"Cat stop your change! There is no immediate danger." Once a Were starts their change it is almost non-reversible. Only the strongest Alphas have the capability to do what Cat then did. She slowed the process and reversed it. Every time she did it she got a splitting headache. I got up from the floor and grabbed a bottle of painkillers out of my bag and a glass of water.

I handed them to Cat as her face shifted back into the form that I liked the most. "Man that smarts! Thank you." She took her medicine and glared at me. "What the hell was that scream for? I thought there was a killer in here or something."

"Through my shield? Please. No, let me show you." I stepped back over to the windows and opened the drape up. Stuck to the window and staring right at me was a man. His face was plastered right up against the window. He was frozen but completely aware. His eyes swirled in panic at his situation. There was another one higher up, all we could see was a foot stuck to the window. I stepped over to Cat's room and peered through her windows and could see another man stuck upside down with his back to the wall just below the one that scared me. A rope dangled down from the roof and was flapping in the wind.

"Are they stuck to your shields like last time?"

"They are. I'm not releasing them without backup. Let me text Nita and let her know. Then I'm going back to sleep." I pulled out my phone and took a picture of the man looking at me stuck to the window like a spider. I gave her a brief run-down of what happened and how many. Just for grins I forwarded the text to Anastasia. If anyone was awake over at the command center, it would be her. I pulled the drapes shut and went back to sleep.

Forensic Tech Commander Anastasia Moondragon was in her element. She and her team had an entire warehouse and manufacturing plant to process and search. While she was pretty sure they had already found what needed to be found, it would give her people some much needed practice. So far this case was boring. She had just finished processing the molding equipment when her phone dinged. Looking at her watch she saw it was five. Way too early for anything official and there were very few that had her current number. She stripped off her rubber gloves and pulled out the phone. Hitting the View Pictures button, she started to chuckle. The candid shot of the man stuck to the window was priceless. The guy hanging on the wall was nice too. Scanning the text she decided to see if Nita had gotten it too.

Anastasia had been alive a lot longer than many Agents in the FBI suspected she had been. She was extra careful to not to fall for the age jokes and games the other forensic techs liked to play. In all of her years she had met and worked with several witches and wizards. Rule one when dealing with magical people was never, ever piss them off. From what she has seen Agatha was not someone to annoy. Tayanita Lowrey should be in the command vehicle if she wasn't taking a nap. For as long as she had known the agent, Anastasia knew she would be working.

Dawn was just under an hour away so Anastasia needed to hurry. As she rushed, she thought about the young witch and Were that started this trek in the wee hours of the morning. Dawn was coming and if she wished for her secrets to remain secret, she would have to hurry. Who knew keeping a secret this long would suck so much? Vampires were in most ways exactly like fiction portrayed them: allergic to sunlight, not fond of garlic, liquid diets, and cold to the touch. Not all vampires are created equal, however. The really old ones were different and very, very rare these days. By tradition and culture vampires lived underground in vast cities, called nests by the other paranormals. They fed only on the willing, not the unwilling. For over a thousand years a special truce had been in place between the vampires and the other para's. The vampires would serve as the diplomats and legal representatives to the para world and give up drinking from the unwilling in exchange for not being wiped out. Magical threats are a real hazard and vampires are very flammable. Blood was supplied through a very intricate system of debts and balances owed. Willing participants could sell their blood to vampires. Debt and obligation is what ruled a Vampire's life.

The really old Vampires ruled the nests with iron fists. It was they who controlled the others' lives. When war broke out, the nests in Germany and Austria chose to help in diplomatic ways but they were betrayed. The very magical people that they depended on to monitor society and enforce the laws turned on them and used them in war. The eldest were trapped inside their own cities. They were powerful enough to resist the Spells being cast upon them but had no way to leave. The same happened in hundreds of other cities as the war widened. Career diplomats were sent out to calm the other races and to request assistance. Much travel was restricted due to the war and Vampires such as Anastasia were trapped in countries they were only visiting. Then the night of the Purge changed everything.

In a single moment Anastasia lost everything. Her family, her city, her country, and her entire purpose in life or in death. The Purge took it all. She had been in Japan to organize a trade deal and then she had nowhere to go. True ancients were in demand to help refugees and take control of cities. She had no real desire to do any of that. Taking careful steps to not be detected she slipped into obscurity and disappeared. Her secrets safe, she changed her name and her life. Many of the older cities on the East Coast were in search of residents so she joined groups of young vampires and blended in. Over fifty years had passed before she found something that gave her purpose again. She took her old name again and joined law enforcement.

She found Nita with her head down on the desk sound asleep. Time was running out, so she had to wake her.

"Nita sweetie, time to wake up." Shaking her slightly the Vampire tried to be gentle. The agent mumbled in her sleep and tried to pull away. Being a bit more forceful she gave her a shake again.

Nita opened her eyes into the face of Anastasia. She jerked awake and checked the time. The Tech commander held up her cell and told her to read her messages. "You got an important one from those two youngsters. They forwarded it to me. I have to go, the sun is rising." Running faster than a human, the vampire spun out of the vehicle and was in her own just as the sun painted shadows upon both vehicles.

Nita pulled out her phone and checked the messages. What have those two done now? She hit view messages and began yelling for some of the other agents. Time for a field trip and maybe a way to get into Emery's house.

CHAPTER 15

I knew we were in trouble when I heard the pounding on the door. My phone had begun pinging at me barely an hour after I texted Nita. The sun was coming up and our FBI keeper was on the warpath!

"What the hell were you thinking?" Nita and two of her agents pushed their way past me into my hotel room.

"Uh, what?" The male agents threw open the drapes and were trying to figure out how to open the windows.

Nita pointed at the windows. "That! Agatha, really? Did you and Cat think I wouldn't be upset? If the press sees that, Washington will crawl up my ass! You are a Witch and Cat's a Were. You didn't have to leave them stuck on the side of the building like a twisted Halloween display! Damn it! You are training to be FBI agents! Where the hell is Cat, anyway?"

I threw a pillow at the sleeping lump on the other bed. "Hey, wake up! We have company!"

"Waaa..t. Company?" Cat sat up and saw the red faced Nita and the other agents and squeaked. She covered back up.

"Now we need to get them down and find out who they are! Can you release them? Please?"

I floated the one pressed up against the window inside and un-zapped him. The others were a bit more difficult, but I got them inside. The one that was upside down was the worst. He was near catatonic having spent nearly three hours upside down with his back to the wall three stories up.

As soon as they could move they began babbling that they were innocent. They weren't killers or assassins. It seemed they were hired to break into our room and offer to hire us away from the FBI. Their employer didn't like taking no for an answer especially from mercenaries. He wanted our services, and he was willing to pay for it a lot. For such a smart man Senator Emery was pretty dumb. He didn't know that I wasn't one of the Russian mercs that everyone used. No one in Washington had a real Council Sanctioned Witch or Wizard working for them.

"You two got very lucky. No one from the press saw anything. Only one guest asked about it and Agent Smith told him it was a new publicity advertisement. Be sure to thank him for that; he saved your ass. If we didn't need you so badly, this might have gotten you kicked out. Next time, think! Promise me you will try to listen?"

We promised her and then ducked into Cat's room to change clothes. I put my special vest and all the gear we were issued on along with my clothes. For once we looked a bit like real FBI agents.

The ride back to the command center's current location was very quiet. The other agents all knew we got read the riot act. I had reactivated my ward to guard the room and left instructions for the maids to NOT clean it. Trapping the staff would not endear me to the hotel. Fergus elected to stay and watch TV all day instead of coming along. I gave him snacks and hay before I left. He could not open the Ward, so room service was out.

Nita called a meeting in the command center as soon as we got back.

"What do we have? Tell me what we know about all three Senators and the Mayor."

"We researched what was available about the Senators. They went to different Colleges in different states in different years. They each graduated with different majors except for the Mayor and Senator Emery, who are both lawyers. The Mayor is a tax attorney, while Emery, when he practices, is a corporate one." Anastasia was on the video screen from her van.

"That's interesting. Find out if either of them have any clients anymore. Go on."

"Each man was married in their early twenties; only the Mayor while he was still in college. Their wives are all educated and from the same schools as their husbands. According to school records they met through the fraternity system."

"Were they in the same frat in college? Many of those do brotherhood events."

"No. Senator Emery is a Tau Kappa Epsilon or TKE. Senator Payne from Georgia is Alpha Phi Alpha and Senator Owen is Sigma Nu. The Mayor is Phi Kappa Psi. We couldn't find any connection between the chapters that links them to each other. Their wives, however, are all from the same Sorority, but from different chapters - and in Mrs Emery's case, years."

"What Sorority do they all belong to?" Nita had a funny look on her face.

"All the wives are Alpha Nu Omega. We checked and their daughters are in the same sorority too. Legacies for the most part."

"Add that factor into your search, see if the men had contact with each other through their wives. What else do we know?"

"None of the Senators became politicians until after they married. They worked their way up the political chain, local to State, until they achieved their positions. All are very outspoken and popular in their States. We have the 'nut files' from each man and there is no crossover. It reads like it's random which is strange."

I raised my hand and spoke. "Agent Lowrey? What about the mothers of the children? Maybe it's not political at all and has to do with them."

Nita smiled at me. "Good question, Temporary Agent Blackmore. Anastasia what do we know about the parents?"

"Senator Emery's daughter has a health condition and is hospitalized at the moment. Her husband was a local mayor in Virginia but was killed in a freak lightning storm. He was playing golf in the rain. It was a few years ago, and it checks out. Senator and Mrs Payne have custody of their granddaughter because their daughter Emily and Benton Walburn, her husband were killed in a car accident on vacation. The Walburns were off celebrating his win in local elections as a city treasurer. Senator Owen's daughter is serving in the Navy as a sub commander. We show her currently on a Top Secret mission. The department of the Navy refuses to release her records to us. We do know that she and her husband divorced after the birth of the child. He is a State Senator in North Dakota. We checked: he hasn't left the State in over a year and has no contact with his child or ex-wife."

Half the people in the room shook their heads. What a douche.

"Like the Paynes, the Mayor and Mrs Wilson's daughter was killed, or at least that is what we think happened. They were on vacation in Florida three years ago. They were staying in Orlando at one of the parks."

The whole room winced. Even me. I remember watching some of it on television. Grandmother told me the rest of what happened. The Magical community has its rebels much as any other communities do. A small group of Wizards and Witches took over one of the Orlando theme parks to protest mundane characterizations of them. The Wizard's World theme park was encased in a shield bubble for over forty-eight hours. By the end of the stand off, all the park staff and half the visitors were dead. Many of them transmogrified into trees or other living creatures. What one magic user does cannot be reversed by another. There is a large exhibit at the Jacksonville, Florida zoo where many of the former victims ended up. They aren't people anymore. The Witches' Council came down hard on the perpetrators and killed them on the spot. Changing people and animals against their will on purpose is against magical law. So far nothing I have done was on purpose.

"So only one parent is aware of the kidnappings? This just gets harder and harder. What about our wall-crawling friends?"

"They haven't asked for a lawyer yet: but one showed up for them. He works for the same firm that Senator Emery is a part of. We got some nice taped video confessions from them before he showed up. Emery was the one that hired them. He has used them before to acquire business secrets according to them. Unfortunately it's all hearsay."

"What about forensics? Did we get anything off the coins or the statues?"

"We have the statues figured out. The spell is used to affect the sense of reasoning and leave the person susceptible to suggestion. For a child, it acts as a lure making them trust a stranger. The coins are demonic in nature. We think they were created in the early part of the twentieth century. Metallic traces show the gold comes from a particular mine in California that was played out by the early 1940's. Similar coins were found during the two previous investigations, but it was not known if they were demonic. Magical support at that time didn't detect anything. The only lead we have is Senator Emery's bodyguard, Aalu Kovacic."

"OK. I will call legal and try to get us a warrant to search the house and bring in Kovacic for questioning. I expect that Emery will have it squashed in minutes of us serving it so move as fast as possible. Agatha? I need for you to do your Demon scan as soon as we walk in. If we find anything it will slow the judge's ruling and allow us to continue."

"Anastasia? Keep digging. We might have an angle with the wives. Keep me in the loop. Now, let's get ready to move, people."

Nita stepped over to where Cat and I were sitting. "Good question earlier, Agatha. How are your studies coming along?" Both Cat and I groaned. We were given tablets filled with procedure that we had to read before doing anything else. It was incredibly boring.

"I know it's a bit tedious but you have to understand procedure. No matter how badly we need you, if we don't follow procedure, valuable evidence could be lost and criminals set free. Think of it as punishment for going back to sleep." She smiled and walked off to make some phone calls.

Cat and I spent the rest of the morning staring at the damn tablets. It was starting to make sense, and we began to quiz each other.

"OK people let's get moving. We have warrants and a very small window to use them in!" Nita woke us up from the daze we were in.

We grabbed our kits and stepped out of the command center and into the bright Virginia sun. We took two teams of agents this time as well as a tac-team. They would stay out of the house and away from us unless there was armed resistance. Cat and I rode with Nita as usual but we had three cars altogether.

"Do we get guns this time?" It was an innocent question. Cat gave me a nudge.

SAC Lowrey turned in her seat and looked at us. Agent Smith was driving. "Do you really need them? I know Agatha can zap someone in a heartbeat and you are faster than most everyone here. What do you think?"

"That would be a no, then." Cat tried to look innocent.

"Good guess, Miss Moore. Don't worry about it. Once you graduate, you will be assigned a weapon and given the proper training for it."

We were traveling much faster this time than before. Agent Smith had explained it to us. The Federal Judge that granted the warrants still had to follow procedure of his own. But he gave Nita time to serve them. Instead of sending them in electronically, he sent a courier to the court. It was allowed under the rules. The Senator's watch dogs wouldn't be notified until after we were in the house. But we had to hurry. We used the emergency lights to clear traffic.

Arriving at the gates to the house we found them closed. We had to use the intercom. Whoever was on the other end of the speaker tried to stall and Nita had to use threats to get in.

"Tell the Senator that if he does not open these gates, I will tell the armored vehicle in our group to crash through them. We are coming to the house!"

There was a click, and the gates opened on their own. We sped toward the house. One of our units was already in place at the rear gate and the armored vehicle and tac-team would stay by this one.

"Nita, I could have opened the gates fairly easily."

"Agatha you are our 'ace in the hole' here. He doesn't know your strength, and it's never a good idea to let the bad guys know all your capabilities."

"I can see that." And I could. At the moment he still thought I was a merc.

The Senator himself was waiting for us as we pulled up. Nita jumped out and handed him the warrant.

"Now see here, Agent Lowrey, I protest this intrusion." He grabbed the Warrant and began reading it.

"Senator, we have both video and eyewitness proof that one of your staff, an Aalu Kovacic, commissioned and received the cursed statues that were used in all four kidnappings."

"Aalu? That is crazy! He has been a member of my staff for almost twenty-five years. Why would he do something like this? Who signed this?" The Senator whipped out his cell phone and immediately made a call.

Nita waved us all inside; we had a job to do.

When we were here last, I had scanned the lower levels and the entrance. Cat and I ran for the stairs and went up to the top. I dropped into my trance and began looking for magic traces.

There were small traces everywhere. All the surfaces in the house were protected against damage and the elements. The first door we came to was the Senator's office. The walls were of the 'I love me' variety and packed with pictures and awards. Cat began taking pictures of the walls. A forensics team came in behind us and started fingerprinting the room. The Senator had a number of active spells in the room. The desk was spelled to prevent scans of the man and deactivate listening devices. A few others revealed illusions, and some looked for hidden weapons. If he worked in here, he was well protected. On the desk were a few magical artifacts that had the look of souvenirs. Nothing showed red to me or set off the bracelet.

There was another office across the hall. Mrs. Emery was a mover and a shaker in charity organizations. Her office walls were not as impressive as her husband's but were still covered with pictures and awards. A shrine of sorts was set-up on a side board. A small pyramid of containers with the words 'Fabulous Face' on the sides stood in the middle. All the pictures on this wall were related in some way to that company. My bracelet twinged when I leaned closer to the wall. I dropped back into my magical sight and blinked in shock. The entire room had a very faint glow all over it. It wasn't a good glow either. I told Cat to photograph as much as she could.

"Girls, we have to go." Agent Smith stood in the doorway.

"Agent we may have found something, this whole wall…"

"It doesn't matter. They revoked the warrant. We have to go right now! The Senator has called the local police to escort us if we won't leave. Let's go right now."

The Agent all but dragged us out of the office and down the stairs. Nita was arguing with a local LEO as we were loaded into the SUVs. Nita threw up her hands and nodded.

"Well that was a freaking waste of time! Aalu Kovacic was not on the property today. He took a personal day or something. Not sure who the Senator called, but he got the warrant canceled faster than we thought he would."

"Nita, we found something in one of the offices." She turned in her seat and stared at us. She made a motion with her hand.

"The forensic techs said they didn't find anything in his office, what are you talking about?"

"The wife has her own office. The door was open, so we stepped inside. The whole room glowed. She had a sort of shrine set up to a company called Fabulous Face. There was a product display and a lot of pictures of the plant and of gatherings. Cat took lots of pictures."

"When you say it glowed, what do you mean?"

"Magic gives off energy; that energy glows to those with magic sight. If your sight is tuned correctly, you can see the glow as colors. I didn't get a chance to see more than the general glow of magic. Does she own a business?"

"Get with Anastasia and dig into that when we get back."

I pulled out my cell phone and tablet and began to research Fabulous Face on my own.

"Ma'am, we just got another message and download from the field team."

"Good, put it up on the main screen and start breaking it down." Anastasia was very frustrated. So far three downloads had been sent and no new information on the Senator. She was starting to think he might not be the guy.

"Have we gotten any information on the women? What about the Sororities?"

"That is the only link we can find: Alpha nu Omega. Ma'am, do you find a bit strange that all its members are married to either politicians or men of power?"

"What do you mean by that, Johnny?"

Jon Carr had been a tech for over ten years, but Anastasia was the only one who called him Johnny. "Emily Payne went to the University of Georgia. They were able to send us records of the Sorority sisters in her year. If you look at the list, they all married men who became either politicians or elected officials." He put the list up on the big screen.

"The entire class?" Anastasia stared at the list.

"All but two. One is in prison and the other died the year she became a sister. The locals ruled it an accident."

"See if you can get the records from that death and the one in prison. This is strange. How's our research into Senator Emery's wife progressing?"

"She's pretty normal. Gives to a variety of charities; the only one that raises any red flags is one of those Save the Orphans campaigns. It raises money for some of the Slavic or Balkan areas. Way too many rebels and anarchists come out of there. Her college degree was Business, and she runs a few non-profits and sits on the board of at least one cosmetics company. She has many business connections that her husband uses. She is definitely the power behind the throne."

"Agent Lowery and the teams are on their way back. Keep digging."

As soon as the cars pulled up Cat, and I jumped out. We rushed to the forensics truck so Cat could turn over her pictures.

"Hey Anastasia? We have something for you." I called out her name as soon as we stepped foot inside the lab. I could see the techs hard at work and the whiteboards were all full.

"Hello you two, staying out of trouble this time?" She peered at up over her computer screen.

"They didn't give us too many opportunities to get into trouble. We did find something interesting though... The Senator's office was clean. He had the usual protections and a few magical things on his desk but they looked like souvenirs or gifts. His wife has an office and the whole thing glowed. I was just starting to investigate when they pulled the warrant and we had to leave."

"That does sound interesting. Wait... you said the wife? Senator Emery's wife?"

"Yes. Her whole office glowed of magic."

Anastasia looked at one of her techs. He nodded at her.

"Ma'am, it might be her and not the husband. It's the only thing that fits. They all belong to the same group."

The Vampire looked at the two of us with a gleam in her eyes. "What did you get besides a scan of that office?"

"I took pictures of all the stuff on the walls and on that goofy altar she had."

"Altar? What Altar? You didn't say anything about an Altar, Agatha!"

Cat handed her a camera disc.

Anastasia projected the images up on the main screen. Very carefully she scanned through the pictures. They were of Awards banquets and what looked like Charity events. The pictures transitioned to a cosmetics factory and cold cream production awards. The 'Altar' was a pile of cold cream jars and some Sorority items. It was interesting that the two were together.

"I did some research on my phone in the car. Fabulous Face is a privately held company. Mrs Emery is listed as the President of the company. Her husband is shown as its legal representation."

"And there is the link to the husband... Dig into that company. I want to know everything you can find. Tear open the Sorority too: members, property, origins, the works. I want it all. Good work, Agatha and Cat."

We continued to stare at the pictures. The ones we could see now were of children and depressed looking villages.

"Who's the boy with Catherine Emery?"

We all peered at the picture.

"Good eyes Cat. Run facial recognition and add thirty years to it. She looks a lot younger in that picture."

"Ma'am, the computer says it's a seventy-five percent match to Aalu Kovacic."

"There is the connection. We have been chasing the wrong Emery. It's the wife not the husband." Anastasia was typing as fast as she could.

"But why? One of those girls is her own granddaughter. It doesn't make sense." I stared at the Vampire. Why would someone kidnap their own child?

"I can tell you why."

We all swiveled to face him.

"Mark, what do you have?"

"I researched the Sorority as you asked. Alpha Nu Omega was founded before the Demon war in the 1930's. At that time it was called a different name. They changed it in the late 1940's. The original name was Beta Upsilon Epsilon. BUE: the Sorority is a Bune cult."

CHAPTER 16

"How?"

"How what? How did they get away with it for so long or how did they do it?" Anastasia had called Nita immediately and told her the good news.

"More like how did we miss it, but those are good too. This is a political nightmare. Our own research shows that these women only marry politicians. They could be everywhere!"

"Agent Lowrey, let's worry about the group here and pass the report off to Washington. Can we do that?"

"Don't tell me how to do my job, Anastasia. But you're right. We need to find the little girls. What do we know about Fabulous Face?"

"It's an American company. For the past five years they have been located in Alexandria, Virginia. According to tax records they employ over five hundred local people in one capacity or another. Everything from drivers to shipping agents. They mix, fill, and ship their product from that small complex of buildings." Up on the screen was an overhead shot of the plant.

I studied the picture of the plant. That was a lot of buildings to search. "Where was the plant located before it moved here?"

"According to tax records they relocated from Meta, Missouri."

"Where the hell is that?"

Nita grabbed a computer and started typing. "It's near Jefferson City. Anastasia, see if they had any disappearances or kidnappings five or six years ago in that area."

"Nita, I will put my people on it. Do you want us to go farther back than that?"

She nodded. "Yes, all the way back to the beginning if you can. Track the board of directors too."

The Vampire nodded her assent and continued to type.

"Do any of the wives have contact with that cosmetics plant?" Nita looked at Jon.

"We have been checking; other than women's makeup that they might have in the house we can say no to that question. There is nothing to connect them to the plant."

"Damn. OK, dig into their husbands accounts. If there is a connection, we need to find it and fast. We still have four lost children we have to find." Nita pointed at me and motioned for me to step outside with her. Cat stayed in and helped Anastasia.

"You told me when you got here that you were having nightmares about the kidnappings. Are you still?" My eyes widened. I barely remembered saying that to her.

"Not last night. Those idiots on the roof prevented that." I rubbed the new bracelet. Since I put it on, I'd been doing that a whole lot. "My foresight is not all that strong. I thought it was my weakest power. I might - might - be able to put together a spell to enhance it. It comes with a big warning though. My off-the-cuff spells have a fifty-fifty chance of going haywire. I could hurt someone by accident or turn some squirrels purple or something."

"How bad are we talking here?" She really looked interested.

I looked off into the distance. I could see the flashing lights of the police units on our perimeter over the fence. I cut my eyes in her direction. "Last time I crossed a rabbit with a deer and made a Jackalope. Actually, I think I made a bunch of them."

Agent Lowrey started laughing. "Change as many rats as you like around here, but try not to get the weasels over there." She pointed over the fence where the News vans still swarmed.

"I'll try it inside the warehouse. The worst that could happen is it burns down. Have Cat standing by to get me out if it goes sideways." I pointed to the warehouse. "Let me get some things from my packs." I headed back inside to get them.

"Agatha, thanks. This might really help."

I nodded. She had no idea how bad this could be. My bracelet gave a little shimmer. It had never done that before.

Once inside I dug into my packs including the one Cat was hauling around for me. I pulled out lavender, more of my special salt blend, chalk, and paraffin. These sort of spells were best done at night but the Gods really don't care. It's the thought that counts.

"What's up Agatha?" Cat sat down next to me as I dug around in the packs.

"Nita wants me to try to enhance my foresight and see if I can get a read on the girls."

"Can you do that?"

"I think I can but I have to cast a spell to enhance my vision. I could call Grams but she wants me to stand on my own. She told me that much last time. I'm going to make one up and give it a whirl."

"Did you warn them? I mean, last time you made some sort of creature."

"Yeah. I did tell Nita. Cat, I really need to do this. We have no idea where those kids are. I need to do something constructive."

Cat patted me on the back. "Just don't make it destructive instead. How can I help?"

I sent her off to Anastasia to find me a few things or some similar I could use. My pack full I stepped over to Nita.

"I have most of what I need. Spells such as this are usually done at night, but I'm going to go for it, anyway. I need to do it outside: the warehouse won't work after all. Can we pull the vehicles around so the news media can't really see what I'm doing?"

"Will you be safe?"

"No idea. I have to call upon some very scary forces to give me what I need. Cat will be helping. I will try very hard not to kill us all."

"Good safety tip there, kid. Don't kill your co-workers. OK; approved. Use the SUV's if you have to."

I stepped back outside and looked at the parking lot. It might be big enough for what I needed. Digging into my bag I pulled out my chalk. I'd bought several of those big buckets of chalk they sell for kids, which was appropriate. Pink and green would show up well out here. I made a mark in the middle of the lot and paced off my circle. It needed to be big. Anything that spilled over could hurt someone or something. I stopped for a moment and centered myself.

My Grandmother is a traditional Witch. She believes that spellwork should be done a certain way and with care. I trained under her for most of my life after I went to live with her. She taught me everything that I know how to do. The knowledge has been passed through our family for centuries. Her style is a blend of ancient, modern, and traditional. What I was about to attempt she would not approve of. Not even a little bit. So I was going to use a tiny bit of ritual magic and draw a protection circle around my workspace: I was that worried.

"Agatha! They didn't have any candles, but I did find the wood for torches. There was a steel bucket in the shop that will work as a cauldron."

"Great! Thanks Cat. See if you can find something to put the torches in: paint cans or something like them, filled with either sand or dirt. Then I need you to move all the cars and extra vehicles along the fence so the news crews have a hard time seeing what I'm doing. Nita approved it."

"What are you doing?"

"Something potentially very dangerous. Don't worry Cat, I'll be fine. This is going to be very hard for you: whatever happens do not cross the lines and enter the circle. Very bad things could happen, both to you and to me. The way the circles work is they protect the caster from the very powerful Eldritch powers that get called up. If I pass-out or faint stay where you are. Promise?"

"Agatha if it's that dangerous…"

"Promise me? I will be OK."

"Fine. I promise. But you better be ok or I'll kill you myself!"

I had to smile at that!

"This is going to take at least an hour to draw out. After you move the cars, leave one out. I'm going to need Fergus for this. Only he can walk through the wards."

I turned away and pulled out my chalk. Very carefully I drew a large circle on the parking lot. Most would use a stick and some string. I used magic, but the result was the same. Then I drew another one a foot larger. On the inside I made one small enough for me to stand in and if I collapsed still not break the circle. Now for the fun part. The incantation and runes. Out of the corner of my eye I saw Cat come out of the warehouse with five paint cans. She set them next to the wood pile and ran toward the command center.

"Nita, Agatha said it was OK to move the cars?"

The SAC was standing staring at the map of the cosmetics plant. "Yes. Get with Agent Smith and he will give you a hand. Can she do what I asked for?"

"She says she can. Did she tell you what might happen?"

"She did. It's a risk but we have to find those girls. What is she doing out there?"

"Drawing a circle. Thanks Nita!" Cat ran outside to the refreshment tent where she last saw Agent Smith.

With his help she got all the cars and other vehicles moved up against the fences. The reporters began shouting questions at the agents. Agent Smith raised an eyebrow. "You know this will attract their attention even more, don't you?"

"I know and so does Agatha, but she can't do this inside the warehouse. She could blow it up."

"Oh. Should we be under cover for this?"

"She told me that she will try her damnedest to protect us."

"You two are really good friends aren't you?" The Agent was taking Cat to the Hotel.

"Yeah; she started as my roommate last year. I think of her as the sister I never had. She is Pack in my eyes."

"That's pretty cool. One of my partners was a Were. He liked to talk about Pack and dominance fights all the time."

"What kind of Were is he?"

"Was: he took out a rogue Wizard two years ago. The wizard had us pinned down behind a fence and Charles changed into his other form. He was a Polar Bear. Charles charged the rogue and took him out."

"How did he die?"

"Lightning strike. The Wizard called it down as he died. Took out my partner and a city block. That fence saved my life."

"Sorry for your loss. He sounds like he cared about you as a partner. I've never met one of the Bear shifters but I have heard they have great heart."

"That he did, little lady. That he did. So what are we picking up here?"

"Fergus. He's Agatha's Unicorn."

"Unicorn? There was a Unicorn in that room? Where?"

Cat laughed. "You'll see."

They pulled up to the Hotel and went inside. The staff was used to agents coming in at all hours and barely noticed them. Cat pulled out her room key card and swiped it. The door unlocked.

"I thought this room was warded so nobody could get in?" Agent Smith looked around as they entered. The TV was on some cartoon about horses.

"It is. I can get through it. Fergus, I know you are in here. Agatha sent me to find you. She needs you for a spell."

"Well it's about fraking time! I've been sitting in here waiting for something to do. It would have been nice to have a little room service but no. Don't bother to feed the Unicorn!"

"Fergus, I promise you if you come with us I will get you a chef salad just like they make at that place you like. Now come on." Fergus stepped out from behind the TV.

"How did you get up there, anyway?" Cat peered at the tall TV table.

"I jumped."

"Agent Smith, this is Fergus." The large agent just stared at the mouse-sized Unicorn

"Is he a real Unicorn?"

"Are you a real FBI Agent? Of course I'm a real Unicorn. Great deductive reasoning there, Agent. Where did you find this guy?"

Cat picked Fergus up and put him in her backpack. "Hey it's dark in here! Damn sneaky cat! I just knew this was a trap."

Agent Smith just stared at her. Cat chuckled. "Agatha carries him around in her shirt pocket all the time. You'll get used to him. He's a bit outspoken."

"A bit? Why does she need him, anyway?"

"I'm not sure. He is her familiar, so it has to be a magic thing. You can ask her when we get back if you like."

"I will pass, I think. I don't want to be turned into some sort of animal for asking the wrong question."

"She won't do that. It's against the Council's rules. Transmogrification is against magical law unless it can be shown to be a true accident."

"Huh. I didn't know that. What I heard was she gave a really good lecture on the paranormal history of the Purge."

"She did, and someone tried to kill her because of it. She is supposed to do a second one on what Witches can and can't do. She is very powerful and the first of her kind to join the FBI. From what I've seen you really need her."

"I can agree with that one. I've been in four firefights that I thought I was going to die in. Magic on our side would be a blessing." We were almost back to the warehouse but traffic was getting worse.

"Damn. Unless you want to be on the News, you might want to duck." The news media presence around the warehouse had tripled in size. Cat ducked down in her seat as they entered the parking lot. Agent Smith moved the car to where it blocked the last part of the fence. I could see Agatha was still drawing in the parking lot.

The outer rim of the circle was almost complete. I had been drawing runes and writing out incantations for over an hour. Once activated, the circle should hold all the energy and magic inside. Should. Magic had a funny way of escaping when it wanted to. I would need to be very careful. All five of the torches were placed and drawn into the spell. I left a doorway between the elements of Fire and Water. I would fill it in when I was ready to enter. I could only draw the inner circle once I was inside it.

I saw Cat drive up and smiled. She must have gotten Fergus. I would need him in his role as a familiar today.

"Hey, Cat! Did you get him?" I stood up from the ground. My legs were starting to cramp up.

Cat unzipped her backpack and looked inside. A voice could be heard from inside. "Did you leave dirty socks in here on purpose? God, the smell is awful!"

"Fergus, quit your griping. Cat was just trying to help. Come out of there, I need you." I reached down and picked him up.

I held him up to eye level. "I need you as a familiar today, Fergus. The extra energy you supply will help."

"What are you trying to do? Since when do you need more power?"

I walked him over to the circle and let him see.

"I need to try to boost my foresight to try to find those girls, Fergus. I created a spell for it..."

"Did you call your Grandmother and ask her for help?"

"No. I'm gonna wing it."

"Try not to change those nice FBI guys into squirrels before they feed me. I'm looking forward to my salad." I smiled. Ever the optimist was my Unicorn. Carefully I stepped away from the circle and over to the command center. Nita was standing against the truck watching me.

"Is everything OK?"

"Yeah. Now that I have Fergus, I need to eat something and then I will be ready. I have everything I need. This might get a bit crazy so be warned."

"We trust you Agatha, just don't turn us all into Jackasses."

Laughing I told her I wouldn't. The cantina truck was parked at a funny angle to block off the news media people. I stepped up to the window and ordered a salad and a sandwich. I wasn't all that hungry but I soon would be. Magic took a lot out of you.

Fergus got to eat his salad, much to the delight of the other FBI agents. Few of them had seen him before. I finished my sandwich and stretched really thoroughly. This would either work or it wouldn't. I had to try. Waving at Cat I called her over.

"Cat, remember: do not cross the lines. If anything happens to me, call my grandmother but I should be OK." She gave me a big hug. I kissed the top of her head and squeezed back.

Then I stepped into the circle and squatted to fill in the incantation words. This was going to be hard. The smaller circle was about ten feet in diameter. The larger almost fifty feet in diameter. It would need all of that to hold the power of who I was calling. Hekate was not a minor player.

On my knees I began closing the inner circle with runes of my own devising. Grandmother gave me a good grounding in ceremonial magic and the Kabbalah. Protection circles I could do. I pushed everything into the exact center of the circle. I needed to be sure nothing broke the circle.

Raising my arms I let out the breath I was holding. Sinking into myself I felt my connection to the Earth and all the other elements. Now it was time to begin. Calling the elements, I welcomed them into my circle and asked them to bless me in my endeavor. I had done this a thousand times in the past. Never had I actually felt the elements join the circle. I felt the circle join and power begin to fill the outer circle. I was going to raise power and use it. There were many Goddesses that would be appropriate for finding lost children. None of them were both a patron of my race and my personal Goddess.

Concentrating on the element of Fire I lit the five torches at the perimeter of the circle. It was time.

"This is the hour of my choosing, my hour of need. I call upon the dark Goddess, she who rules the moon and all Witches. I call upon Hekate to attend and bless this location with her spirit." I stood in the center of my circle with my eyes closed and called out my prayer to the dark Goddess of Witchcraft.

"What is she doing?"

"I've seen her do this before. She's calling the quarters. The elements are called the quarters: Earth, Air, Water, Air, and Spirit. Once they join the circle, she can raise power. She will then call upon the Gods and use some of that power."

Cat and Nita stood inside the Command center in the doorway. They watched the sky grow dark and the wind begin to howl. Thunder rumbled in the distance. The wind was quickly screaming through the fences.

"Agent Lowrey! We just received a tornado warning from the weather service! They say they have never seen anything like this before!"

The sky tuned night black and dogs could be heard howling in the distance. Wind began to swirl around the circle. Bits of paper and other debris were sucked into the maelstrom that was forming in the parking lot. The effects of the storm began to lessen, but the sky remained dark as night. Agatha could be seen standing with her arms to the sky in the center of what looked like a tornado trapped inside the circle.

As the day turned to night, Cat continued to keep her eyes on Agatha. For just a split second she thought there was two figures standing in the center of the circle. A large gust of wind almost made her lose her balance. When she recovered Agatha stood there alone. The winds began to dissipate, but the Sky continued its darkness. Agatha was no longer standing. She lay in the center of the circle.

"Cat, she's down! She could be hurt!" Cat grabbed Nita by her arm and would not allow her to go over.

"No! I promised her that we would not break the circle. I gave my word. We will stand here and watch. She told me that bad things would happen if the circle broke. We will stay right freaking here!"

SAC Lowrey tried to pull her arm away, but the small woman's grip was rock hard. Small she might be but Catherine Moore was an Alpha and she could be as strong as she needed to be. The sky slowly began to lighten, and the winds dissipated. Agatha was still not moving. Cat gritted her teeth and gripped Nita harder. She'd promised. Finally Cat could see Agatha move her arm and sit up.

Chapter 17

I woke up to Fergus standing on my face kicking me in the nose. "Quit faking and wake up. Agatha, you need to wake up!"

"What the hell, Fergus? Get off me!" I sat up and rubbed my head. Ouch that hurt. The last thing I remembered was talking to Hekate. It had to have been a dream, but I would almost swear that the Goddess herself answered my plea. Wearily I stood up. I could see Cat and Nita waving at me from across the lot. I rubbed out a section of the chalk circle just to be sure before stepping across it. The torches were all out but I also carefully rubbed a door into the second circle. Trust your instincts and not your eyes is one of Gram's sayings. It was just a variation of better safe than sorry.

"Are you alright?" Cat came over and gave me a big hug.

"I'm fine, I think. My head is killing me! Let's get inside before I forget. I think I might know where they are." We ran to the command center; well, I walked fast.

All I could see were the looks of shock and awe on the faces of my fellow FBI agents and techs. Many of them had seen what I had not. The tornado and darkness of the sky. Otherworldly forces had been called, and I was the herald. I think it had finally hit home to many of them just what a real Witch could do.

Nita was all business, which was good. "Did you get anything?"

I nodded my head. I thought back to the vision or dream that I'd had.

"The room was dark and a musty scent filled the room. Small sharp flashes of light shone into the room from broken pipes in the overhead. Ice cold water dripped from the ceiling and ran down the metal walls. Parts of pipes and electrical tubes ran across the walls and into the floor. I could hear what sounded like fans or propellers running at top speeds. Ear deafening machinery would roar to life on either side of the metal box every few minutes. I could scream but the sound would not be heard over the roar. Looking through the gloom I could see a tiny girl in each corner of the room. We were each crammed into the corner, embracing what security we could find. I no longer heard the cries of 'grandma save me' coming from the others. I knew she wouldn't come. She's the one that put me here. Closing my eyes I said another prayer for grandpa to save me. He was the only one that loved me."

"That's horrifying! Could you tell where they were?"

"No. But I could hear the roaring. It was like the sound a wind tunnel would make. They are alive that's all that matters." I played the vision back in my head. I was missing something, I just knew it.

"We just need to find them and to prove the women did it. Making it stick to Catherine Emery will be the hardest part."

"No. It won't. She has betrayed the love and trust of a child. A family member who she was supposed to protect and care for. Demons aren't known for rewarding those who fail them. Add to that a vengeful Goddess and she will receive what she deserves. Hekate will make sure of it." Those listening took a step back from my sepulchre tone.

214

Cat told me later a chill ran through the place as I spoke. I only knew that the Goddess was not amused.

"We have to catch her first. Agatha take a look at the factory, look for anything familiar." Nita looked around the room, everyone had grim faces. "What do we know about the history of Fabulous Face?"

"I had my people search every database and records center we had access to and a few we don't. They traced the company back about twenty-five years so far. We have a pretty good picture of what they do. It seems to be a five-year cycle. In the first year the plant moves in and sets up operations. They use existing facilities or on one occasion build their own. Ninety percent of the company are local hires. Community governments love them until the fifth year rolls around. Twenty-five years ago they rolled into Trophy Club, Texas, and set up shop. The area was new and construction was booming. On the outskirts of town they rebuilt an old TQB parts facility. Local labor was hired and production was at full steam by the second year. As the town began to boom so did the plant. In its fifth year everything changed. Reports were filed by the board of directors outlining a re-consolidation of assets and hardship rules for the plant. They claimed it was due to production losses. The workers were puzzled as the plant was in full swing including a lucrative third shift." Anastasia paused and looked to left and nodded.

"The FBI was investigating a kidnapping of a girls sports team that year. It was suspected that they were smuggled through Dallas-Fort Worth but we could not get a handle on it. Half the team of eight was recovered on the Mexican border, but four of the girls were never found. Our files show it as an open case. Later that year the plant moved.

We show a discernible pattern. The plant stays for five years, in the fifth year several kidnappings occur in the area. The plant closes and they move to the next State. We have them in Fox, Alaska; Wilson, North Carolina; Elgin, Illinois; and Meta, Missouri. They pick small to middle-sized cities to avoid notice. We are still searching for more of their previous locations."

"Anastasia are all of those locations confirmed?"

"The ones we named, yes. We have other possibles. This is potentially a huge case. I am preparing information for the brass."

"You said that their last location was in Missouri? Call the closest FBI office and have someone talk to plant operations or the owners of whoever is in there now. Find out from them what was missing or strange when they took possession of the factory. It may relate."

I stared at the aerial view of the factory. I saw nothing that screamed wind tunnel to me. All I could see were buildings. I looked up when Cat came back inside the truck. I hadn't realized she'd left.

"Has, uh, anyone looked at the parking lot lately?" She was pointing toward where they had been congregating.

"What's wrong Cat?" Nita looked concerned.

"Trees. Really big trees." She sat down and stared at me.

"Nita, does this thing have exterior cameras?" I pointed at the big screen.

"Somebody hit the button for the cameras!"

The picture on the screen changed and we could see outside. All around where my circle was drawn trees were

216

punching through the concrete. They looked like Oak and Ash trees. They were growing at an accelerated rate.

Everyone turned and stared at me. "I did say there might be some consequences. At least I don't see any purple squirrels this time."

"OK everyone, back to work we have children to find. Agatha do you need a moment?" I nodded at her and moved to step outside. Cat smiled at me and stood up to come with me.

Outside the temperature had changed. It was at least twenty degrees cooler than it had been earlier. I guess Goddess visitation carried with it low pressure systems and trees. I pulled out my cell phone and gave Gram's a call. She would want to know about this.

"Agatha, child, are you alright? I received a message from the Council about a huge surge of magic in Virginia. Was that you?"

"Yes, Grandmother. It was. I'm on temporary assignment; I can't discuss the details but I performed a spell to enhance my foresight." I had to hold the phone away from my ear.

"You did what? Agatha, that was extremely dangerous. You especially run the risk of burning yourself out. Obviously it worked or you would not have called me. What happened?"

She sounded concerned, but I was very hesitant to tell her about the Goddess. It was almost private. "After the ritual, trees pushed their way through the concrete and now ring the place where I performed my magic. Grandmother, I created a grove! We need to save this place from destruction. Can you contact the Council for me and tell them?"

There was a brief silence.

"Child, for once you had a positive aftereffect to your magic! Did it enhance your foresight also?"

I described in general terms my dream. She told me the Council would be notified. After I hung up, I stared at the new Grove for several long minutes.

"Aggy, I saw her."

My eyes widened, and I turned toward Cat.

She too was staring at the Grove. Without looking at me she continued to speak. "It was during the ritual. A tornado formed directly over you and the circle. It was all I could do to keep from falling and I thought I saw another figure in the circle with you. I tried to get a closer look but a sudden gust of wind knocked my feet out from under me. When I looked back the other person was gone, and you were lying on the concrete." Cat sniffed. I could see tears rolling down her cheeks. "I followed your instructions, but I thought I'd lost you..."

I leaned over and gave her a big hug. From what I knew about Were Packs closeness was encouraged between Pack members. "Cat, you should feel honored. She would not have allowed just anyone to see her."

"When all of this is over will you teach me about her?"

"Of course. I would love to." We stared at the trees for a few more moments and then went back inside. We had a kidnapper to find.

"What do mean they are under arrest?"

"Sir, from what they admitted to the lawyers we sent, there was some sort of Ward over the entire hotel room. The team stuck to windows and remained caught there until the FBI got them loose almost three hours later. They had already told the Feds who'd hired them before our man got there."

"Dammit! What the hell do I pay you for? Did they at least make the offer to that Witch? Her magic is exactly what I need around here." Senator Seymour Emery could only glare at his damn people. If they would only do as he asked! If his stupid daughter Margaret hadn't called the FBI, his men would've found her by now. He had promised he would find Elizabeth,, but she didn't believe him and called them in. Those freaking FBI agents couldn't be trusted to find Elizabeth. Only he could do the job properly. There was no secret that money couldn't find the answer to. You just had to know the right people.

"Sir, according to some of our people in Washington she's not a mercenary. She's the FBI's first Council-approved agent. This one isn't interested in money."

"Everybody is interested in money! It's what makes this country great. If she's from here, trace her family. Find an angle and push it; I want her on our team by week's end! Now, how goes the search for little Elizabeth?"

The tall man paled. He and his team had found nothing. The Senator had offered a huge reward of five million in cash for information that led to either the kidnappers or his granddaughter. But every underworld contact had come up with the same thing: nothing. His men had tried to find out what the FBI knew and had come up empty.

"Sir, we don't have anything more than the FBI does. They found the supplier of those statues before we could and took possession of the entire complex. But the workers there don't know anything. Most were illegals to begin with. Our contacts tell us the owner was a lowlife that worked with the Cartels to smuggle in drugs or whatever. They won't be releasing him anytime soon."

The Senator kept his cool but his face got more red with each disappointment. "What does the FBI know? Why did they search my office? Have we been able to hack them to find out?"

"No such luck on the hack. They have one of the best techs in the business working for them. The past two document searches have been foiled by that new Witch. Our mole inside the Justice Department says they had evidence that one of your servants is the one who had the statues made. They think you are behind the kidnappings for some political reason."

"Who here would do something like that to a child? If you can't find out, buy someone then. Everyone has vices or secrets. Find one and pay them off. I need to find her. Tell our people to block any other such inquiries and notify me the details of any potential warrants."

"Yes, Sir. We will do what we can." He watched the old man as his servant helped him up the stairs. The Feds had the edge here, and he knew it. But the old man had a point. Everyone has a secret they want kept hidden.

Senator Emery stared out the window of his office. He'd made a promise to his daughter and he would live up to it if it was the last thing he ever did. She needed to understand that he was a man of his word regardless of the law and those who made the rules.

Even if some of those rules had been made by him.

The command center was humming when we got back inside. More information about Fabulous Face had been discovered. Each time they'd moved was after the disappearances of children. The board members also changed from location to location for the most part. Though Catherine Emery had been on the board for more than thirty years. Every disappeared child had some connection to the ANO Sorority. Both the FBI and local LEOs had missed that fact. But then, it was so far fetched they had not been looking for it. Agents in Missouri had located the tiny town of Meta. A pet food company occupied the cosmetic company's location now. A short list of building modifications and repairs had been sent. Many people in the town had vivid memories of the cosmetics company and were still bitter about its relocation to another State. Agents had been sent to the other locations as well, but in most cases too much time had passed for any useful information to be gathered.

"Agatha, here is the list from Missouri of the changes and repairs that the former plant needed. It's not much but it might spark a memory. See if anything leaps out at you, please." Nita handed me a clipboard with hard copy attached to it.

I took the information and found an unoccupied desk near the air conditioning unit. All this computer equipment needed to be kept cool or it would shut down.

The desk I chose was the coldest in the room so it was naturally avoided.

The construction list read like a contractor's dream. When Fabulous Face had pulled out, they literally ripped things from the walls instead of carefully removing them. Doors were damaged; over forty walls had holes that needed patching; tile floors were scraped and needed replacing; and several windows were shattered. The company kitchen was in terrible shape and the walk-in had been completely removed. The factory floor and production areas fared better than the corporate levels. Machinery had been carefully removed and packed up. Some of the electrical grid was messed up and needed to be replaced. Also, one of the industrial air conditioning units was vandalized and needed to be replaced. A copy of the police report was included.

The AC I was sitting next to kicked on with a roar that for a moment sounded like a wind tunnel. I froze literally and figuratively. I cocked my head to the side and considered the report again. I studied the police report. Was it even possible? That was all I could think of.

This desk didn't have a computer on it. I went over to the main desk and Nita.

"I think I have something. Can you pull up the overhead shot of the plant again?" The screen changed, and I studied it carefully.

"Did you find something?"

"I'm not sure it's even possible, but it's the perfect hiding place."

"Where are they?" I now had the attention of the room.

"I think they are inside one of those industrial Air Conditioners. If one was hollowed out, could a small group of children fit inside?"

"Jonathan, pull up pictures of industrial AC units. Mark, get on the phone and find someone who works on those things and ask how much room they have inside. Call the damn manufacturer if you have to..."

I broke in. "Nita, I know where they do the ritual too. The records show a lot of damage to the buildings, but most was superficial. There was one thing missing: the walk-in cooler from the kitchen. It is metal and has a large locking door. They design those things to have drains built in and to be capable of being washed out with a high-pressure hose. Plus they go together like a jigsaw puzzle and are easily removed." It was the only place the ritual could have been done. Anywhere else would have left traces.

"Good work, Agatha! See if you can pinpoint that location along with the probable location of the girls. I suggest you study overhead shots and see which fans are not in operation. I will call the brass and get a warrant."

Cat joined me and we began to study the multiple overhead pictures of the plant. We had three possibles by the time Nita got off the phone. "OK people, we have one shot at this. Senator Emery is the legal representative at this place and he will take this as a personal attack. We need to find those girls:. That is the priority! If Aalu Kovacic or Catherine Emery are spotted, do not pursue alone. We do not know what capabilities they have. To make any sort of case, we have to find some trace of the girls. The warrant allows us to visit the kitchen walk-ins and any industrial air conditioning unit. If we have to follow the rules, so do they. All agents go gear up."

"Do Cat and I get a weapon this time?"

"I can't do it, Agatha. I do want you to wear vests and armor. You need to be identified as being with the FBI. If you were at least Probies I could get away with giving you a gun. But I like my job too much to risk it. If you are attacked, you have my permission to fight back in your own ways. That is the best I can do."

"That sucks!" Cat looked pissed.

"She has a point. If we got hurt, it would be her ass on the line. That amulet I gave you should protect you from most things magical, but remember what I told you to do. Doesn't your War form make you mostly invulnerable?"

"It sort of does. Not many of us can assume that form for very long."

"Can you?"

Cat made a face. "I can. I haven't in awhile. It's sort of a dead giveaway to others that you are an Alpha. I have only changed into that form twice."

"OK, I've got your back. Don't be afraid to change if you need to." She smiled at me and we ran for the armory.

The armory truck was the most heavily armored of all the vehicles with us. They had our armor laid out and waiting for us. I thanked the armorer and began putting the vest and body armor on. "Are you going to be able to wear that and still keep from crushing the life out of me?"

I had completely forgotten about Fergus. To call the Goddess I had used all the energy stored within him as my familiar. It had been just enough. The little terror had been sleeping it off until now.

"I'm sorry Fergus, I clean forgot. Let me see if I can fix it." I called the armorer over and explained the situation. Like many of the mundanes he could not take his eyes off Fergus when shown him.

"Miss Blackmore, that armor is not designed to be modified in the field. We would have to have the manufacturer bend a plate and make a hollow compartment for your... companion."

"OK. So this is my assigned suit? No one else's?"

"Yes, that is correct. It is the one assigned by command specifically for you." The puzzled tech still stared at Fergus but he nodded yes.

"Cat, can you fix this please?" I handed the armored vest to the Were. Using her fist Cat pounded out a compartment for Fergus in the vest.

"We might have to fiddle with the straps but that should work."

"Thanks Cat." I smiled at the man as I put Fergus away and strapped on the vest. The cosmetics company was about ten miles away so we had to hustle. We all knew we were running out of time.

Chapter 18

Serving the warrant was easy. The gate guard was a rent-a-cop who when confronted with over thirty heavily armed FBI agents complete with a Tactical Team folded like a sheet of paper and allowed us inside. Nita strode into the main building to present the warrant. The rest of us spread out to look for our targets. The mechanical area was in the rear of the facility. Twenty large AC units sat on pilings pushing air into the building. Their roar sounded exactly like the one from my dream. According to the pictures, two possible units were on this side of the section and the last one at the very back. Cat and I would take that one and the trio of agents with us would take the closer ones. We all had radios, but the noise was so loud I doubted we could hear them.

I sensed, rather than saw, the bolt of energy that just missed me. I'm blaming the bracelet, but it twinged just in time for me to change direction. The bolt hit one of the AC units and caused it to arc electricity into the air. Both Cat and I spun to the ground and looked for the caster.

Hiding behind the last unit was the missing Aalu Kovacic. He had gleaming red eyes and a fireball in each hand. He tossed one at me and I pushed Cat out of the way. I felt it slide off my shields. "Cat, get the girls to safety! I will handle this guy!"

Taking a deep breath, I engaged my shield and threw a fireball of my own at the cultist. Saying a silent prayer to my Goddess, I hoped that no hostages were in any of these units as we threw fireballs at each other. Sparks and melted droplets of metal filled the air. This guy was starting to piss me off! My fireballs only glanced off of the machines his melted holes and sank into the asphalt with a demonic glow. I hoped that Cat was having success.

"Sir, we just received a call from Catherine. The FBI is at Fabulous Face. They just served a warrant to search the place."

The Senator sat upright. "What? Now they are harassing my wife? Get the car we need to get there and stop this nonsense. They need to be searching for my Granddaughter. I will have the head of whoever is in charge of that group. Call Catherine back and tell her I'm on my way!"

Cat stumbled as she dodged another fireball. Agatha was deflecting most of them but the cultist was getting close to her. She interpreted that to mean she was close to the girls. The last bank of machines was in the corner of the walled area. The center machine had a large padlock on it. That had to be the one she was looking for. Keeping one eye on the magical duel she tried to pull the lock off, and it was stuck. Glancing away from Agatha she concentrated on the lock. It was an older style but it wouldn't break no matter how hard she pulled. The metal of the air conditioning unit groaned under the pressure she was putting on it. Cursing, Cat began stripping off her armor as fast as could. Reaching down inside of herself, Cat called forth her warrior form.

With a rumbling growl, a large Bigfoot-sized humanoid cat hooked it's four-inch claws into the edge of the door and ripped it off the AC unit. Four tiny shrieks of terror could be heard from inside the unit.

"Doonnn't beee afrrraaid! Ressscuuee." Cat's voice was very deep but could be clearly heard. A tiny head poked out of the hole and let out a squeak when it saw Cat. Four very wide-eyed little girls could be seen through the small door. "Pleeaase cooome wiithh meee. Saaafffe." Retracting her claws Cat carefully helped the girls out of the large metal container one at a time. A fireball, deflected during the battle came arcing over the units and hit the retaining wall with a loud bang. All the girls jumped, but it didn't scare them. Cat remembered where the cars were and motioned for the girls to step back. She charged the wall with all of her strength and battered a hole through it.

If the members of the FBI tactical team reacted to an extremely large Cat-creature bursting through a wall near their cars, they never said anything. Leaving half the team to guard the gate and vehicles, the rest rushed over and helped the girls get out of the enclosure. Explosions from the battle could now be heard by all as it drew closer. Cat turned and went to go help her friend.

<<<>>>

The cultist was relentless. His fireballs were more powerful than mine and he knew it. I was trying not to throw anything more for fear of hitting the girls. I could hear Cat's growls behind me so I knew she may have found them. I intensified my fire and started calling up balls of electricity. I was hoping he was a one-trick-pony, and that was all he was able to use against me. I threw the first electro ball and hit him through his shields! He staggered and responded with a flurry of fireballs that came at me like a shotgun blast. I ducked and threw up my arms to shield my face. I thought for sure I was dead.

I felt the heat of the fireballs as they struck my arms but there was no pain! Opening my eyes, I could see a faint shimmer that covered my arms and upper body. A strange shield was coming from the bracelet on my arm. I raised my left hand and threw one of my fireballs at him. I heard a loud roar and one of the largest warrior form Were I had ever seen attacked my opponent, Aalu Kovacic. He was hit from behind as three-inch claws ripped through his body. As he went down, another rain of fireballs was directed at who I assumed was Cat. I spoke the word "hlíf" and covered my friend with a glowing shield. I threw a freeze ball at the cultist and he froze for all of ten seconds. He was trying to crawl away as I hit him again with an electro ball.

"Cat, is that you?" The large Were nodded its head.

"Yeesss. Nooottt Usseett tooo tallkkk."

"Thanks for the assist. He was starting to get through my shields." I nudged the man with the toe of my shoe and we could hear a groan. He was still alive.

"Whhhyy nooot freezzz?"

"I was worried I would hurt the girls. Did you find them?" Cat nodded at me and turned to point. I could see part of the hole in the fence that she made. Neither one of us had handcuffs or even zip ties to lock down this guy. He was bleeding very heavily and would need a trauma team or some sort of express healing. While I have some skill with healing, I never took any sort of Hippocratic oath. Scumbags don't get medical care from me. Cat nudged me

and almost knocked me over. She pointed at my radio
which I had completely forgotten about.

SAC Lowrey and her team found the cafeteria and
kitchen area fairly easily. The warrant only allowed a
search of two specific areas; any industrial air
conditioning units and metal walk-in's and freezers. She
kept this part of her team together, they were not to
wander off. She had just gotten to the kitchen and ordered
them to search when she heard a voice behind her.

"Agent Lowrey I protest! This is retaliation and bad
business! Why are you harassing my wife and I when you
should be tracking down who kidnapped my
granddaughter?"

Turning around she found the Senator and Mrs. Emery
standing in the doorway accompanied by two of his
bodyguards and two of the executive staff.

"Senator we are searching for your granddaughter. Mrs.
Emery, I have some questions I would like answered
please?"

"Catherine don't say a word! This woman and her
campaign to ruin us stop now! I have called our associates
and they are putting a stop to this." The Senator beamed
at his wife who only smiled.

Nita frowned at the Senator. "Sir, your wife is involved
in this up to her neck! Your man Aalu Kovacic is the one
that ordered the creation of the statues given to the
children. We have a video of him paying off the model
maker and inserting Demonic artifacts into them to set

the spell. Magic associated with Demonic energy was detected in your house."

"Aalu is involved? Ridiculous? All of our servants are checked very thoroughly, and he has been with us for years. You're lying."

"Are we? What about this place, Fabulous Face. Why does it move every five years? There were four kidnappings in the Jefferson City area in the months before the move, all were children of politicians and all were sorority sisters of you wife's national organization. Five years before that a similar crime was committed in Texas. Every five years children are kidnapped, and this company moves right after it happens. We have records that go back thirty years or more. Why does it move around so much?"

The Senator looked at his wife who smiled at him. "Honey, make them stop saying bad things about me and my company!"

Senator Emery looked past the fake smile that his wife had and really looked at her. "Catherine is any of this true?"

"Seymour why would I hurt little Elisabeth? We are a family, don't let these people take all of that away from us!"

He looked at Nita. "I agree with my wife Agent. I refuse to believe you. This is nothing more than a put-up job to accuse me or my wife of something we did not do."

"Agent Lowrey? We found something in the walk-in you need to come look at!"

"Senator I have to go see what my people have found if you will excuse me?" Nita turned and walked toward the back of the kitchen.

The Senator started to move toward the kitchen also when one of the other agents told him to remain where he was or he would be charged with obstruction. Several more of the kitchen staff and a few executives drifted into the dining room. They, along with those already there, began to rubberneck and watch what was happening.

In the kitchen, the walk-in door was blocked open and several agents were outside it, bent over a bucket throwing up. "What is it?"

One of the senior agents motioned for her to enter. Pushing through the PVC strip curtain Nita entered the large commercial walk-in. The front section contained racks filled with food used to feed the workers. Beyond the racks of meat, vegetables, and prepared food lay the real horror. The thick insulated walls were carved with the runic or Goetia script. Idols on pedestals lined the walls. Statues of horrific demonic beings. thirty in number were atop the pedestals. A massive altar built from what looked like red basalt covered the entire back wall. A painted representation of Bune hung as a backdrop. Over a hundred jars lined the back of the altar, each contained a heart the size of a clenched fist. As Nita drew closer, she could see that bones made up much of the construction, they framed the stonework and were used as altar pieces. Human skulls were used as cups and pools of blood dripped from the surface of the structure. The dismembered corpse of what appeared to be a young woman was laid out on a low table nearby.

Nita felt bile rise in her throat but refused to allow it to go further. She was an experienced agent and refused to show any weakness to her team. "Call in the Tac-team we need to lock this plant down. No way anyone was ignorant of all of this! Start taking pictures! Photograph everything!" She turned and walked back out into the mostly clean air of the kitchen. Yelling at the milling FBI agents she pointed at the kitchen staff. "Start arresting everyone!"

"Senator you and your wife are under arrest." She motioned to one of her agents to take control of him.

"On what charges? I will have your badge for this! False arrest is a serious charge!"

Nita leaned in toward him. "Senator we will start with murder, kidnapping, and conspiracy to commit murder, and end with obstruction of justice, and interfering with an official investigation. What is in that cooler over there will have you in the deepest, darkest hole our government can find!"

"Whatever you have found is planted! This is a conspiracy to defame the Emery name!"

"Senator, Demon worship is not illegal in this country but murder and kidnapping are. There are over a hundred human hearts in there. You will be known as one of the most prolific serial killers in the world! Handcuff him and read him his rights."

"Demon worship? What have you been smoking? My family puts the B in Baptist! This is a trick! Catherine tell them I had nothing to do with any of this!"

Nita heard a crackle and her radio beeped at her. She grabbed her microphone and replied to the broadcast. "Go ahead." She listened for a moment and replied. "Call an ambulance and get him checked out, have Agatha put a freeze on him and then find me in the kitchen. Tell her that I need them both here. What about the girls? Great, have the local field office send reinforcements and put them on twenty-four-hour watch in the children's ward."

Looking at the stunned Senator, Nita started to talk. "Good news Senator. Your Granddaughter is safe along with the other three girls. Once the doctors finish examining the girls, we will place them under protective custody. Your man Aalu Kovacic is also under arrest. He was seriously injured by a very angry Were, but we think he will survive."

"You found Elizabeth? Where was she?"

"Don't you know? She was here at the plant the whole time. Out in the AC pen, there was a hollowed out unit. All four girls were in there. I assumed you knew since you protect this place stringently."

"She was here? At the plant?"

"Senator I'm starting to believe you. I'm still going to book you and prosecute you but maybe you didn't know that this place is run by a Demon Cult. Let's ask your wife, shall we? What do you say Catherine about all this?"

Mrs. Emery stared at Nita and smiled. Her eyes had a tiny red glint to them. She pursed her lips and looked at her husband with disdain. "Such a little man you are. Too good to see what is right in front of you. All that eloquence, all that power, everything you always wanted and you never once asked how. How is it that a man who wasn't a good lawyer who barely passed the Bar could sway his district into electing him to a public office? Never once did you ask me how? Ah, tradition is such a good thing." Catherine's smile was almost angelic but not quite.

"Catherine, what are you saying? Surely you didn't take little Elizabeth. Why?" The Senator just stood there with his mouth open.

"Silly man. Everything has a price. You should know that by now and don't call me Shirley." She began to laugh, and it was not the laugh of an old woman. "Being human has been so enlightening. All your petty desires and whims. So easily manipulated. Each time we give a little you take more and more. Before you know it we are the one making all the rules. It has been so easy. The master only takes a few and only once a cycle. Parents can always have more children but true power comes but once a lifetime. Time for this charade to end." Catherine Emery seemed to grow in size before Nita and the other agent's eyes.

The old woman's eyes turned bright red and large claws sprang from her fingertips. She slashed the agent holding her arm across the chest as she lunged toward Nita.

Nita pulled her weapon and began firing at the Demon that had appeared in her midst. She yelled at the other agents to protect the civilians.

Catherine Emery was no longer human, or she had never been. She began to laugh as the bullets penetrated her skin and went out the other side. Red could be seen in the holes but no blood. "Civilians? There are none of those here! Bune is all here." The factory workers and kitchen staff now Bunis, all drew weapons and began to engage the FBI agents directly.

"Bune needs a sacrifice. He prefers the youth of the world but you and your agents will suffice for now." The

236

Demon woman had her husband by the arm and was holding him up in front of her eyes. "Goodbye, Seymour." She ripped his head off and threw it at the agents firing at her.

Every agent carried blessed icons that according to those who make the rules were supposed to be effective against Demonic activity. Whoever came up with them was crazy because Nita's men were losing and losing badly!

Nita tried to rally her men and women behind the serving line, but their weapons were having no effect against the Demon. Several of the Bunis had already been killed. The former factory workers were not bulletproof like their leader.

Cat and I heard cries of "officer down" on the radio and struggled to get to the rest of our team. Like flicking a switch almost every factory worker inside the gates was transformed into a Bunis, a follower of the Demon Bune. The large group that had been milling around in the front were now attacking our gate unit. That unit had taken the children away and was only at half strength. Murmuring a prayer to Athena I uttered the word "stǫðva." The charging crowd froze for just a moment then they continued their charge. My eyes widened. That spell always worked before! I tried to remember everything that Grams had taught me of Demonkind.

The agents at the gate opened fire and dozens of the Bunis were down writhing in pain. I braced myself and said another prayer this time to Persephone to open the way for those swayed by evil. Pulling reserves I didn't know existed I began throwing fireballs at my new enemy even as we ran across the courtyard. Cat, still in her massive Warrior form reached the Bunis before I did and began slashing and biting at will. The Tac-team at the gate started picking shot as they tried to keep some of them from us. I was in full battle mode using spells I was taught but never ever used.

The crowd of over a hundred was slowly whittled down to dozens as I froze, burned, and blasted my way toward the gates. Cat protected my rear slashing anyone that got near me.

"Agent Blackmore! Thanks for the assist!" The combat armor-clad agent was one I had met before.

"Where's Agent Lowrey?" I looked around for Nita.

"We received Officer down calls from her and her team. The last location had them in the cafeteria. They reported that the Senator and his wife were under arrest and a murder victim was discovered. They went dark after that."

"Do we have a backup?"

"We have requested it but it may be a while. I mentioned Demons over an open channel." All I could do was shake my head. Stupid.

"OK. Cat and I will go try to find them. Please don't let anyone escape."

"Come on partner. I motioned toward the front entrance." Cat ran ahead of me and crashed through the glass doors. Weres.

Chapter 19

The lobby was deathly quiet. Only the sounds of glass falling could be heard inside. Outside we could hear the Tac-team doing the clean up followed by the occasional shot. Demons were illegal in every country on Earth. Here in the United States, they could be worshiped, but never, ever raised. We have had a shoot-on-sight order for demons, and those possessed by them since the 1940's. Many of those exposed to demons during the war had to be put down. Thousands of innocent civilians were abused and tortured in the camps to make them susceptible to possession during that war. Only a few dozen survived it. Many went insane. Laws were passed outlawing attempts to even try to save those poor tortured souls. Grams told me those in our community tried for years to 'fix' some of our own damaged by the war. Finally, the Witches Councils signed one of the few documents that actually agreed with mundane laws. Death to Demons.

A small tear rolled down my cheek. I just helped kill several hundred formerly innocent people. That is what exposure to evil does to you. I reached up and wiped my cheek.

"Cat. That amulet I gave you should protect you from a demon attack, but you only have thirty seconds to escape. If I go down save yourself." The immensely large were came over and waved one finger in my face scolding me. "OK, message received." I gave her a hug.

We ignored the upper levels of the building and carefully made our way toward the company cafeteria. In the distance, we could hear what sounded like screams and gunfire. We needed to hurry but not at the cost of our own lives. Athena only knew what was up ahead of us.

The first body we found was one that we knew. Agent Smith would never again tell his stories to another new agent. A quick look at the body told me that he was attacked from the rear and probably never knew what hit him. Damn Bunis! I would remember him in my prayers and bless him on his way toward the afterlife. Something made a loud roar that echoed through the halls. We could now hear the occasional gunshot. I grabbed Cat's arm as she tensed to run. "Don't get killed. I want my friend back later." The large creature that was my friend nodded and charged toward the sound of battle. Bracing myself I ran after her.

SAC Tayanita Lowrey and what was left of her team were in big trouble. They had been forced back through the kitchen to the large walk-in. The former Mrs. Emery was now a huge demon. Its surviving Bunis were attacking with guns, knives, and clubs in waves. Nita was down to only a few rounds for her pistols and was now armed with a Cultist's spiked club. The demon had stopped attacking directly after Nita burned it with a handful of the anti-demon measures. The agents had almost none of those left but the demon didn't know that.

"What's our ammunition status?" She looked at her weary, blood-spattered men. Only Rodriguez was without a wound.

"Ma'am, we are down to less than four a person. We have all acquired melee weapons and are prepared for another attack."

"Do we know how many of them are left?" Nita remembered taking down at least six with her gun and another four in hand-to-hand.

"Not sure, Ma'am. We each accounted for at least two or three. I don't believe there can be that many left."

Nita glanced at the grisly display behind them along the walls. No one here wished to end up in a jar.

"Start putting a group together to guard the doorway. Plan for a backup team to take over. We have to hold out until we are relieved or dead. No way am I willingly being a sacrifice for that thing out there."

The agents gathered at the door before opening it. Nita gave it a shove and braced for the attack. They were greeted by roars and screams that didn't sound like the demon.

Cat burst into the cafeteria to find a large demon surrounded by broken and bleeding bodies. Bunis surrounded their Mistress and attacked Cat immediately. She dove into them slashing with her large claws. Bodies and parts of bodies flew in all directions. The demon saw the deaths of many of its loyal followers and bellowed out a roar of outrage. Cat answered it with a roar of her own.

I arrived, carefully stepping over the remains of an agent and what looked like the head of Senator Emery. It couldn't have happened to a nicer guy. Cat's roar reminded me of what mundane scientists believe a Sabertooth lion would sound like. All they had to do is ask her.

What was once Catherine Emery was in full battle mode. I watched as skeletal wings forced their way out of her back and flapped trying to lift her into the air. The demon slashed at Cat and tried to grasp her fur. Cat responded by slashing back and kicking with her feet. They were evenly matched for the moment, but Cat only had supernatural strength, and not demonic magic to back her up.

"Fergus I will need all of your strength for this." The Unicorn for once didn't add his opinion. Even he knew I needed all my concentration for this.

Muttering a prayer to Hekate I launched a flurry of fireballs at the few remaining Bunis in the room. The demon screamed louder as the last of its nearby followers were incinerated. Its attention shifted toward me, allowing Cat to slip off to the side to heal her wounds. I followed my attack by hitting it with my electro balls. The demon shrieked, but the balls had little effect.

"You should have taken my departed husband's money little witch. You would have been a fine asset to the cause. You still can be. My master grants much for so little. What makes you the happiest little witch, riches, power, or is it carnal pleasures? I can grant you much."

I didn't fail to notice that it kept referring to itself and not Bune. From the little reading available I knew Bune was a jealous Duke of Hell. He would not share power with a lower underling.

Casting another freeze spell I ducked to the right to gain another angle and launched a plasma ball at the demon. The freeze only worked for seconds, but it was long enough for the plasma ball to hit and tear a hole in the demon's defenses. It ripped half of one of its wings off.

The demon's shriek of pain shook the building. Earth and fire could hurt it.

Cat recovered from her wounds and charged the demon from behind, her claws ripping off the other wing. She received a slash in return from the demon's right arm. Cat's warrior form snarled its challenge and waded into battle again.

Hearing sounds of battle and explosions, Nita and what remained of her team staggered out of the cooler into the kitchen. Blood and body parts littered the remains of the industrial kitchen. Corpses lay in heaps from the mad charges that attempted to overwhelm the FBI agents. Flashes of bright light could be seen as the agents crept to the counter and looked out into Hell.

A monstrous WereCat in warrior form was battling the demon toe to toe. Their pet witch, Agatha, was in full battle mode tossing balls of fire and electricity at the former Catherine Emery. The agents watched in alarm as the were was thrown clear of the demon. The witch cast a freeze spell followed by balls of flame that scored on the demon blowing off a wing. The were attacked again taking care of the other wing.

Nita knew the two couldn't do it alone.

"Cat," I yelled at my friend. The demon was pressing at me again and I threw up my arm to shield praying that the bracelet came through for me again. A small shield stopped the demon's claws and deflected them. I used my telekinesis and pushed the demon away from me. I didn't have a choice. My magic alone wasn't enough to defeat it. I needed to call for help and risk my very soul if I lost. But first I needed to get the team out.

"Cat" The Were shook off the latest hit and looked in my direction.

"Get them out! I need everyone clear."

Cat launched herself over the counter and landed in front of Nita. "Coomme wiitthhh meee."

Nita stared at the incredibly large were. Cat had streams of blood pouring from her side coating the matted fur with even more blood. The swiftly healing cuts were cut to the bone. Nita was surprised she was still standing. She turned to her remaining agents. "Gather everyone up and follow Cat, she will get you out."

"Ma'am come with us!"

"No, Agatha was entrusted to me and I will stay to help her." She felt a large hand on her shoulder and was nearly thrown to the floor as Cat gave her a pat.

Everyone ducked as a random fireball crashed into the kitchen. The demon was now using magic against Agatha. Cat grabbed one of the wounded agents and tossed him over her shoulder. With a jerk of her head, the were led the survivors out of the cafeteria.

Knowing that Cat would get our team out I concentrated on fighting the demon. I tried to marshal my magic and save power. In my head, I worked on creating a spell that could neutralize the demon's power and destroy it. The spell I imagined used control I didn't possess, but I was going to go for it, anyway. Whoever said life was easy!

I murmured to Fergus to hold on. Digging deep into my reserves and pulling from Fergus I said a small prayer to Hekate. She is the Goddess of Witches and a protector of Women. If anyone deserved the justice of the Gods, it was this beast in front of me. A great deal of blood and pain was on its hands.

I reached into the pouch at my waist and pulled out a small handful of my homemade grenades. Now was the time to use them. I said. "Sǫk." That code word said in the old tongue with a tiny bit of magic activated the powerful weapons. I threw my first one as a test. The resulting explosion blew a table across the room and forced another shriek out of the demon.

The first grenade was soon followed by another and then another. There was a method to my madness. With each explosion, I was harvesting a tiny bit of energy. Another goal was to clear as large an area as I could. My consciousness wasn't really here as I followed the fault lines and down to the nearest conduit coming up from the magma core of the Earth. The last thing I wished to do was cause a volcano to erupt in the State of Virginia. The Witches Council would not be amused. Even as I threw another grenade at the demon, I sensed a Dike and a Sill underground coming off a main magma pipe that would do nicely. The Dike was part of an ancient volcano that never 'popped' into existence. Like a plumber I connected to the Sill and created my own pipe running it up through the cracks in the ground left by earthquakes. I needed to be extra careful to not make it permanent.

The demon was starting to gain ground on me I ducked behind an overturned table and threw a few of my dwindling grenades at it again. "What's the matter, little Witch? All out of magic? My master can help you with that. With his assistance, you could control the Witches Council and rule. Does that sound like something that you would like?"

Not being a mercenary was an advantage in a situation like this. Many would have taken the deal by now. Power can be very seductive. You have only to look at my Aunt Camilla to see that. It was almost time to end this. I had three magic grenades left. I ran to the left drawing the demon toward me. Marshaling my magic I mumbled a few words of power and threw the last three grenades. As they exploded, the demon shrieked a curse and crashed into some of the tables. I had managed to lure it to the hole I created earlier. I sent a blast of magic downward and pulled, praying that nothing bad happened this time.

Nita watched Agatha battle the demon across the cafeteria. She seemed to be driving it toward the hole she created on the floor. The witch looked tired as she blasted the demon time and time again with small rocks that acted like grenades. There was a large explosion that knocked the demon down into the shallow hole. It shrieked and thrashed on the floor. Tables, chairs, and bodies flew everywhere. Agatha pointed her arms downward and appeared to speak to the ground.

There was a loud rumbling and then a small explosion. The concrete floor in the cafeteria split open and large chunks fell backward. Molten lava poured from the hole in the floor.

It was all I could do not to fall flat on my face I was so tired. I pulled almost the very last of Fergus's energy and used my telekinesis to keep the demon pinned to the floor. The lava coated the demon's legs, and it shrieked and screamed in pain. Kicking its legs to try and fight free, forcing droplets of molten rock to fly through the air. I raised my arm to shield, and the bracelet came through again. My magic was almost gone as the lava coated the demon and filled in the hole. Its body covered, only the demon's head was free as it screamed its hatred and spite to the heavens. Hurting from the strain I directed the lava to return to the Earth and sealed the hole. Virginia had not had an earthquake lately so the cracks in the Earth were not large or conductive. Magic being what it is, I prayed it would work. My last fleeting thought was that the demon wasn't dead yet as I passed out. I completely missed Nita walking over with a butcher knife from the kitchen and finishing the job.

Chapter 20

My head was killing me. I could almost swear that Fergus was kicking me in the forehead. "Fergus stop it or no more hay."

"Hey, don't pick on Fergus, he's a cool little guy." That voice was definitely not the Unicorn. I opened my eyes. Nita was standing over me smiling.

I reached up to rub my eyes. All I could see were spots interspersed with a double Nita. Blinking a few times I cleared them. "Hey."

"Hey, yourself. Are you awake now?"

"I think so. Where are we?" I was flat on my back on a not-so-comfortable bed staring up at a white ceiling and walls.

"You are in a local clinic that was just down the road from the plant. Nice job on the demon by the way."

"The demon! It's not dead, the head, did someone chop the head?" Holy crap if that thing got out again I don't think I could take it again.

"I took care of that little detail for you. Next time don't pass out. You did good work there Agatha. What made you think of using lava?"

"Earth and fire seemed to hurt it. It was all I could think of. Even then it was incredibly hard. I didn't want a volcano rising just outside of Washington. Are the kids OK?"

"They are. Cat got them to safety and they are in a local hospital being evaluated. The last report I received was that they suffer from dehydration and are a bit hungry. The cult only fed them bread and water."

"Did we get all the Bunis? I took out as many as I could." I could remember hitting them with fireballs.

"We think that the ones here are taken care of. My boss is both happy and unhappy. We took care of the incursion here, but exposed a potential horde of problems." She frowned for a moment.

"The Sorority?"

"Got it in one. That mess is being evaluated on a level higher than I can access. I was told to only worry about this issue. Once you are up, we need to finish clearing the cosmetics plant. How do you feel?"

"Like a herd of Unicorns are stampeding through my ears. I'm fine. Where's Cat?"

"She is back at the plant climbing the walls waiting for you. Something about taking care of her Pack?"

My cheeks reddened. "Yeah, I'm one of the first Witches to be part of a Were Pack."

"If anyone can pull that off you would be the one. She is a force to be reckoned with. Her warrior form is awesome! What does she shift into?"

"She didn't do a full shift? Get her to show you sometime. It's a surprise." I sat up and the herd of Unicorns went away in my head. The room spun for just a moment. Swinging my legs around I started to stand and promptly sat back down.

"Stay seated for a minute. You need to let your body rest."

The room finally stopped spinning. I looked down at my body and all I could see was a white gown. "Uh, where are my clothes?"

"They had to peel the armor off to check you. I wouldn't let them cut your clothes off. Damn doctors get off on ruining them that way. You were only exhausted not hurt. You do have some bruises that look painful, but they say you will be fine."

"Thanks. Where are my clothes?"

Nita laughed and pointed to the chair next to the bed. Everything was laid out in small piles ready for me.

Nita left the room while I got dressed. I found all of my things except for Fergus. I could only imagine the trouble he was getting into in the hospital. My bracelet was still on my wrist the doctors must have been surprised they couldn't remove it. I flashed back on that final battle as I dressed. I was lucky. So very lucky that the demon didn't kill me or the lava flow stopped when it did. I made a mental note to pray to Vulcan during my prayers tonight. I carefully strapped on my body armor. All that was missing was my helmet but it should be around somewhere. I gathered my hair up and tied it into a ponytail. I needed to find the Unicorn.

Nita knocked on the door as she stepped inside. "Ready to go?"

I was sitting on the bed tying my boots. "I am. Where's Fergus?"

"I'll show you. Come on." Nita motioned for me to follow her. The clinic was smaller than a hospital but it had most of what was available, just less. I heard voices and laughter up ahead.

Fergus was in rare form. He was holding court on the coffee table in the waiting room. To hear his version, he defeated the demon all by himself. Pretty good for a hero the size of a mouse. It was time to rain on his parade.

"Fergus!"

The Unicorn froze and looked up at me. I smiled at him. "How's it going hero?"

"I was just telling my new friends about the battle to save the city. Fighting off hordes of demons is hard work."

"Interesting, how much you could see from inside my body armor where you were safe. Are you ready to go? We still have lots of work to do." I held out my hand for him.

I thanked the doctors and staff and walked out under my own power to our SUV. "I can't take you anywhere, hero. Did you have fun in there?"

"Of course I did. You missed it, Agatha, they opened up your armor, and I started talking to them. One of the nurses fainted right there in the emergency room. It was awesome!" I had to laugh at him and his antics.

"Well, we have a lot of work left to do before we can go home." I climbed into the car and we headed back. Nita told me on the way that reinforcements showed up about a half hour after the death of the demon. So did the press. The call on an open channel attracted them like flies to honey. The local police were all that was keeping them out of the crime scene. Pundits were already mourning the loss of Senator Emery. Details had not been released about his wife, yet.

The cosmetics plant was hard to miss. Flashing lights were everywhere. Hordes of news media and gawkers stood in groups everywhere. That didn't even include the relatives and loved ones of those who worked at the place. Most of those would never be coming home. Demon incursions here deadly for all involved.

"You better duck down if you don't want news exposure."

"Thanks, Nita. I forgot." I slid down in my seat to avoid being seen. The media knew I existed, but I didn't want the attention right now. It was too soon.

We passed the security cordon and entered Fabulous Face's grounds. The forensics lab and command center trucks were already set up and agents could be seen tagging and marking the dead Bunis on the ground. The ground was carpeted with them. I was almost sorry for them. Evil was very pervasive in each of those people and it allowed the demon to get to them somehow. Nita pulled the car around the front of the command truck out of sight of the majority of news media. According to what Nita said on the ride over at least one news helicopter had been confiscated for breaking the NO-Fly zone above the plant. A demon incursion was big news.

I stepped out of the car and was immediately embraced by one-hundred and fifty pounds of Cat. "You're back!"

"Hey, Cat. Are you alright?" She pulled away from me and stared at me.

"Me? You are the one that took down the demon and passed out!" Her face was serious.

"Cat, it's OK. I just overextended myself and passed out. Nita got me out."

"Don't. Ever. Do. That. Again. Understand?" Poking me each time she said a word she got closer to me and gave me another hug.

"I understand. I'll try not to let it happen again."

"Good." We then both burst out laughing.

"OK ladies. Let's get to work, shall we? Agatha you ready?" I nodded. We stepped over to the tactical unit and armored back up.

"While you took your nap, Agatha. We brought in more troops and secured the area. We have begun tagging and bagging the Bunis out here and by the AC units. No one has gone inside since I left carrying you."

I nodded. "Let me run a diagnostic spell and see if anything trips it." I concentrated and felt myself slip into the spell easier than before. Something to be said for practice makes perfect. There was what I associated with demonic activity around the Bunis bodies. I expected that. What I didn't expect was the lack of anything else. They had been very careful to keep any trace from the buildings themselves. It made me wonder about the walk-in cooler. That might be why they use it.

I opened my eyes and related what I saw to Nita. She grabbed her phone and called Anastasia in the forensics truck. They talked for a moment. I could see Cat nodding too. Freaky were hearing.

"Anastasia says that might be possible. Many companies use magic to evaluate things. They were very careful. She thinks the cooler may have been taken from jobsite to jobsite rather than start over each time."

"Then we need to go see for ourselves."

"Let's go," Nita called to a tactical team standing by and an even dozen of us entered the building again.

There were a few bodies lying in the lobby. They looked to be Bunis that ran from our units and bled out where they lay. We followed the hallway toward the cafeteria. I could remember chasing after Cat through this very hall racing to save Nita and the team. This time we checked every room, closet, and crawlspace. It took time, but we had to be sure. The cafeteria doors were smoke-blackened and twisted. They looked as if they were hit by more than one fireball. Tables and chairs were tossed like playthings everywhere. Bodies and parts of bodies were burnt and shredded all over the floor. Toward the center of the room, the floor was melted and piled with rubble.

I had to be sure and stepped closer to the demon's death ground. Crimson streaks covered the pinnacle of the mound. A blood trail of drops led off toward the door.

"I cut off the head with a butcher knife. Anastasia has it for study. It was still screaming when I cut it off." Nita was behind me staring at the mound. I patted her arm.

"Sorry, I passed out."

"Don't be sorry. Without you, I would be dead over in that hell-hole of a cooler with what was left of the team. Let's check it out." She led us past more dead Bunis and into the kitchen. I never came this far.

The area around the cooler was a charnel house of death. Nita and her team had literally piled them up outside the cooler. The smell of death was strongest near the open door. Readying a spell I stepped inside followed by Cat.

I could sense the evil inside. My bracelet gave off a shiver that I was beginning to associate with demonic activity. The altar loomed across the back of the cooler. I could see all that Nita had described except for two things. The painting and the statue were gone. "Nita?"

Nita and two of her team stepped into the cooler. "I don't see the statue you mentioned. Is anything else missing?"

The painting, the statue, and all of the other demon statues were gone. The jars containing the hearts were all broken and scattered on the floor. I wanted to destroy the whole place but procedure must be followed. We needed to search the rest of the building.

The upper floors yielded nothing. Offices and shipping rooms were empty of life. It was if the people just walked off the job and either disappeared or attacked us.

"Nita, there were hundreds of people at work in this place. Where did they all go? Does this place have a basement?"

According to plans submitted to the city, it was supposed to. Access was supposed to be available via the freight elevator at the rear. None of the elevators even showed a lower floor. The emergency stairwell was finally found hidden inside a janitor's closet.

"Guns up, there could be anything down there!" Cat volunteered to go first but Nita held her back. She had specialists for that. The tactical team went in first. They threw flash-bang grenades in to clear the room and then charged in. It was several moments before we heard garbled cries of "clear" come from the team.

Our first clue something bad was in the basement was when we passed one of the younger agents puking in a corner. I could smell decomposition as we opened the first door. We had found the missing workers. It was here that those non-Bunis ended up. Imagine the worse thing you can imagine that humans could do to one another and that is what was in that room.

Each body would need to be cataloged but our job here was done. Cat and I had seen too much and been a part of too much over the last few days. It was time to go back to Quantico.

The ride back to school was anticlimactic, no helicopter this time. We were almost scarred by some of the things that we witnessed inside that cosmetics company. I would never look at cold creme again the same way. Both Nita and Anastasia swore that many more lives would have been lost if we had not joined the investigation. I kept running every decision I made through my head trying to see ways I messed up or could have done differently. It hurt that so many of the people I had come to know had died or been disfigured. Agent Smith was a huge loss for Cat. She had bonded with the older man. Cat told me she intended to look up his former partner's family and describe the man's death. It was a were thing.

Fergus was in a good mood unlike the both of us. He was loose inside the car and was starting to get on my nerves. "Fergus calm the hell down!"

"Hay! Hay! I'm getting Hay!" He was doing a little dance across the seats.

"Dude, take a chill pill. We need to get settled and I will get out the good stuff for you. OK?"

"Hay is good!" I looked over at Cat and she just laughed.

"Did someone give him some wacky weed or something?"

"I think he's just happy to be home."

"I guess. Are you OK? You have been a bit quiet."

"Just thinking. I need to work on my fighting skills when in warrior mode. I can see times when I should have changed. Agatha, I know you are second guessing yourself. Stop it. You did way better than they expected you to. Next time they will respect you more."

"I hope so. I really do." I rested my head on my hands as we drove onto the Marine base that was our temporary home.

Director Mills was waiting for us in front of the administration building. We got out of the car and thanked the driver who brought us here. He tried to lift the bags out of the back but Cat had to help him.

"Welcome back ladies. I'm not going to ask if you had a good time. Nita called me the moment you left her. Are you OK? Still want to be FBI Agents? I will understand if you have changed your minds."

Cat glanced at me. "No, Ma'am. We haven't changed our minds. Evil like that has to be fought."

"Good. I thought you might like to take a couple of days off and then on Monday resume classes. The instructors have been holding off on tests until you could return. Remember operational security when discussing the assignment you just completed. The news media has published a great deal of information, but so far Washington hasn't confirmed or denied any of it. Do not be the one to do it first. Allow them to make that decision.

Witch or not, they would never trust you again. Keep that in mind." She started to step away and stopped. "One more thing. I took the liberty of informing a friend of yours that you were back." The Director pointed to her left and climbed the stairs into the building.

We both looked to our right and yelled. Chuck was standing there with a huge smile on his face. He ran over and gave both of us a huge hug.

"Hi, Chuck how's class?"

"Crappy without you two! It's all over the news. Was it really a demon incursion? Are we safe?"

I looked at him and nodded. Reaching over I placed a finger against his lips and shook my head, no talking.

We had only been gone three days, but it seemed a lifetime. They were some of the longest working days in my entire life. I knew that in the future I would look back and laugh at having to work this hard. Our return was not a secret, and many asked the very questions the Director said they would. We stated OPSEC rules and denied everything like we were told to do.

In Washington, the existence of a demon cult was not a new thing. Hundreds of those existed. What sent a shockwave through the establishment was the fact that many of their wives and mothers might be members. One of the biggest cover-ups in history began that night. Records were sealed and documents were signed.

The National organization of Alpha Nu Omega put out a statement condemning it's former Board member Catherine Emery, and those radicals associated with her. How dare anyone accuse a young women's Sorority of demon worship? Lawsuits were prepared and lawyers hired. Any news agency that broached the subject was hit with legal action immediately.

None of that mattered to Cat and I. We had school to finish and another year to plan for. I was hip deep in school work trying to get caught up. We were only gone for three days, but I had what felt like three weeks worth of work to study for. I blame Nita and the Director. They ratted me out to the police procedures instructor, and he piled on the work. Never again would I just go back to sleep after catching the bad guy. I looked up when Cat came in and tossed her books on her bed.

"Hey, Cat. How did the study session go?"

"I think that instructor is an idiot. Since when do we try to capture cultists? Hasn't he ever had hordes of crazies trying to kill him before?" I laughed at her. Our perceptions of things had changed a lot.

"You just like him because he's cute. But I understand. Remember most of them only hunt mundane criminals. We are the demon hunters now."

"Bite your tongue right now Aggy. You and I both know we don't want to do that our entire time in the FBI. I'm starving, want to go to Fergus's favorite place for dinner?"

"That sounds like fun. You have Chuck's Riviera keys again?" Cat nodded and held them up.

"He won't miss them. Hey did Fergus like the gift I gave him?"

"You gave Fergus something? What is it?" I took a couple of steps toward his barn.

"I found one of those ponies he likes so much. I stuck it in his barn."

As I neared the barn I could hear faint music playing it was Barry White. Then I heard what would scar me for life. "Hey baby, come here often?"

Cat and I laughed as we grabbed our purses and ran from the room. No way were we staying for that! Anchors a Weigh here we come.

In a dark basement of a clothing manufacturer, shadow covered figures gathered around a makeshift altar. A gruesome blood splattered painting hung on the wall in a place of honor. The worshipers were few in number but they would grow. There were many that sought power in the misnamed City of Angels. Hell was home to stay.

SNEAK PEEK
MAGICAL PROBI

Black and white police cars lined the street, and the entire front of the place was taped off. News vans and onlookers rubbernecking blocked the streets. It was a good thing I cleaned up the RV because now they were focused on us, not the crime scene. Local officers directed us to the best place to park, and Jack maneuvered his rig into place.

"Now, let me do all the talking. This has the potential to become very high-profile. I've already requested assistance from the local office." His tone was all business now.

"I understand. What will they be doing?" I asked.

"We have a lab in here, so I asked for a tech and some investigators. Experience with this has shown they will either send their best or their worst to help me. I'll let you figure out which they send. It's a thing of pride and glory for many of these locals. They want to do the investigation and bask in whatever media attention they get."

"Why? We all work for the same agency, right?"

"It's politics, Agatha. The entire Bureau runs that way, unfortunately. I try to stay out of it as much as possible. My advice to you is to do the same. Let the locals take the credit. They usually will anyway. You cannot control what they do unless DC gets involved. If that happens, they will be the ones taking credit for your work. Stay in the shadows."

"Saying that sounds like you just gave up Jack. Are you sure that's the best way?"

"Sorry, kid. It's just my experience with the whole thing. Don't worry about it for now. I'm the Special-Agent-In-Charge, so I will take whatever heat comes our way. Try to stay out of the way of any political issue that comes up. Now, since we have been requested, we will be in charge here. I try hard not to run roughshod over the locals so be nice. Get your spells ready I have no idea what awaits us inside. The report only said magical death."

I grabbed my bag off the table and slipped my Glock into my shoulder holster. Regulations required me to be armed at all times, but I didn't like wearing my gun while we drove. I'm, sure I would get used to having it eventually. I didn't foresee using it much, but I was an active Agent now. "Fergus be good and watch the RV." I stepped out into my first real assignment as a Probationary Agent.

One of the local police lieutenants was waiting for us as soon as we opened the door.

"Thank god you got here quick!"

Jack stuck out his hand and shook the man's hand. "Hello, Special Agent Jack Dalton. Why? What's happened?"

"The chef here was world famous. His death has attracted international news media, and they are swarming all over the place."

"You are keeping them out of the crime scene?"

"Of course we are! It's just become a real circus. Chef Robbie Lash was a big name around here. He had two different shows on the Eats network."

Jack glanced at me and shook his head. I kept my mouth shut. "Wonderful. Do you have any leads on your end so far?"

"Not really. We have copies of the security camera feeds, and our techs are running them. So far nothing. You have to see the scene to understand. We've never seen anything like it before."

"OK. Make sure we get access to those tapes. I have a few more Agents on the way so watch for them."

We pushed our way through the crowd of newsies and ducked under the yellow caution tape. The restaurant was done in a French Provincial style and was very fancy inside. The front doors had heavy cast iron handles and hinges. A large oil painting of the Chef was in the front entrance. I had recognized the name; Grandmother watched his shows.

"The scene is in the kitchen. We tried to leave it as is."

"Did the coroner already remove the body?" The young officer froze at that. He stopped again and just stared at us.

"Didn't you get a description? The body is melted to one of the tables. We have no idea how even to remove it much less see how it was done." He pointed to the swinging door I assumed led to the kitchen.

The smell is what struck me the moment I stepped into the kitchen. Grandmother's kitchen always smells of spices and citrus. This one smelled of death and pain. Several officers were standing around staring and a police photographer was puking in a bucket. Not a good sign.

Spotting the sergeant in charge Jack tapped him on the arm. "Excuse me, Sergeant?"

"Feds?"

"Yes..."

The Sergeant barely spoke to us. He yelled at the officers to clear out. "The scene is all yours." He turned and left in a hurry.

I finally spoke. "That was rude of him."

Jack nodded his head in agreement. "Typically they don't like us, but I agree with you."

We both stepped around into the main part of the kitchen line and saw what had the locals so shaken up. Robbie Lash was literally melted into the metal table. The cutting board and table top were part of him somehow. It was like a gruesome statue. The upper half of the Chef's body was metallic and the lower half flesh. At first, I thought it might have been a spell gone wrong but as far as I knew Lash was mundane.

"Have you ever seen anything like this before Agatha?" Jack looked over at me. I had bent down and was looking at the underside of the table. I could see the other half of the Chef's face impressed into the metal.

"No. Not at all. I was thinking it could have been a spell gone horribly wrong, but he wasn't a Wizard. Or at least I didn't think he was. I need to do a diagnostic spell. Hold on a moment."

Surprisingly I wasn't grossed out by the dead guy stuck in the table. I think my experiences with the Demon Cult last year broke me of that. It was nasty but bearable. I said a prayer to my Goddess and focused my will on the diagnostic spell I had learned. Using what a gamer would call my mage-sight I glimpsed a brief magical world in the kitchen.

"Jack he may not have been a magician, but someone or something sure was in here." I opened my eyes and stared at the Agent.

"What do you mean?"

"Just about everything in here has the glow of Magick to it. I need to walk around."

I began following the magical traces on all the appliances. Even the oven had a glow to it. Grandmother had warned me about zapping mundane building items. Usually bad or unexpected results occurred when we tried to enhance those items. Too many Magick users had been swayed by the movie industry to attempt a flying car or magical bed-knob.

The Magick seemed to be concentrated on the coolers. The door to both the freezer and the walk-in glowed brightly in my sight.

"Over here Jack. The coolers glow like they are on fire." I pointed at both the large metal doors.

Remembering the report from last year he voiced my worries. "Do you think it's Demonic?"

"The colors aren't the same for Demon activity. That door just felt evil. I don't get the same vibes from these." I slipped on some rubber gloves just to be sure and reached for the door.

Out of the corner of my eye, I saw Jack reach for his weapon as the door opened. Nothing leapt out at us. No creepy clowns or demonic visages decorated the inside of the door. I stuck my head through the vinyl strips and looked in. I saw a light switch and flipped it on. The shelves in the cooler glowed with Magickal light. Uh oh.

"Jack I think I know what killed the Chef."

"Did you find something?" Stepping into the cooler with me, Jack looked around at the bins of fruits and vegetables.

Reaching into a bin, I held up a piece of fruit. "This is a Fae apple. I think our Chef pissed off the local Fae and they killed him for it."

"Fae? You mean like fairies?" He looked at me like I was crazy.

"Yes. They do exist. Just about all the fruit and vegetables in here are from their gardens. Either Lash had a contact, or he stole all these. Stealing from the Fae is a death sentence. They take offense easily."

"Wait, you're saying the Fae are real?"

Like it? Check out Book 2 Magical Probi
Here on Amazon.com!

Author Notes

I had the idea to do this series a few months ago. I bounced the idea off my wife. She doesn't read my other stuff because she isn't a fan of Science Fiction. Paranormal however is in her wheelhouse. I contracted for the covers with fellow Author and designer Heather Hamilton-Senter. I realized after I sent off the information I didn't even have titles for the books. I brainstormed up a few and fine tuned them with my wife.

My schedule said that I was supposed to be writing and finishing the New Athena Lee Book 10 - War to the Knife at this time. I have half the book done at this writing. Boredom has set in and I'm burning out on the SF stuff. It happens. I needed something else to work on. I was on my way to pick my wife up from work and had a wild hair. What if I wrote a prequel to the Paranormal Series? More of a way to relieve the boredom I wrote 10,000 words in 24 hours. Each time I finished a chapter I dropped it to my editors. When I was done so were they. I bought a pre-done cover and threw it up on Amazon.

I sell fairly well in the SF market. But this little 55 page book blew all of that away. In two weeks Born a Witch sold over 1200 copies worldwide. Readers using Kindle Unlimited read over 72,000 pages on their Kindle readers. It was a double number one book in two categories for a week! It passed some traditional mainstream authors such as Grisham and even George RR. Totally blew me away. So I dropped everything I was working on including the New Athena Book and started this one up. I really hope you enjoyed it.

My plan is to finish up the Athena Book next. I have a great many people waiting for it. I will then dive into book 2 of the Federal Witch series.

Later? I have another Athena Universe book due. Tisiphone and her friends have a trip to make.

Next year will be very busy with Athena, Agatha, and the CATTs. Expect to see more of both series along with a few new things. Lots of new ideas came about this Fall. I have a new non-Athena Lee SF series planned. It will be lots of fun and I hope you stick around to experience it with me.

I have tons of ways for you to follow me. My Blog is the biggest one (https://tspaul.blogspot.com/). https://tspaul.blogspot.com/ I post tons of fun stuff there every few days.

Next we have BookBub

(https://www.bookbub.com/authors/t-s-paul)and

Goodreads

(https://www.goodreads.com/author/show/15054219.T _S_Paul) both of these sites have my books and will notify you if I put up new stuff. There is of course always

FaceBook.

(https://www.facebook.com/ForgottenEngineer/)

I post fun things there too. If you are lucky I can be found there for chat sometimes.

Finally, I have a shout out to the 20bks to 50k Facebook group. It was created as a place for Authors to share information with other Authors without the BS that other forums have. They have been very supportive.

Read and Eat Cookbooks

Badger Hole Bar Food Cookbook

Athena Lee Chronicles

The Forgotten Engineer

Engineering Murder

Ghost ships of Terra

Revolutionary

Insurrection

Imperial Subversion

The Martian Inheritance - Audio Now Available

Infiltration

Prelude to War

War to the Knife

Ghosts of Noodlemass Past

Athena Lee Universe

Shades of Learning

Space Cadets

Short Story Collections

Wilson's War

A Colony of CATTs

Box Sets

The Federal Witch: The Collected Works, Book 1

Chronicles of Athena Lee Book 1-3

Chronicles of Athena Lee Book 4-6

Chronicles of Athena Lee Book 7-9 plus book 0

Athena Lee Chronicles (10 Book Series)

Standalone or Tie-ins

The Tide: The Multiverse Wave

The Lost Pilot

Uncommon Life

Get that Sh@t off your Cover!:
The so-called Miracle Man speaks out

Kutherian Gambit

Alpha Class. The Etheric Academy book 1

Alpha Class - Engineering. The Etheric Academy Book 2

The Etheric Academy (2 Book Series)

Alpha Class The Etheric Academy Book 3 - Coming soon

Anthologies

Phoenix Galactic

The Expanding Universe Book 2

Non-Fiction

Get that Sh@t off your Cover!

Don't forget to check the Blog every week for a New
Wilson or Fergus story.

(https://tspaul.blogspot.com)